A HAUNTED HOLIDAY IN HILLBILLY HOLLOW

BLYTHE BAKER

∽

'Tis the season to be haunted...

When Emma volunteered to help out at Hillbilly Hollow's annual Christmas Garden event, she expected to spend the holidays stringing lights on trees and selling hot cocoa at the ice skating rink.

But that was before a dead man was found in the reindeer pen. It was before a ghost visited Emma, demanding justice. And it was way, way before Emma wandered into a creepy old Victorian mansion to look for a murderer.

Now, with the town on edge and the Christmas Garden facing what might be its last year, can Emma catch a killer and bring back the festive atmosphere at Hollow Heights Park before the event is ruined forever? Or will Christmas Day find Hillbilly Hollow facing its most haunted holiday ever?

∽

1

I made my way across the dew-soaked backyard, past the leaning outhouse and around the chicken coop. Rounding the corner of the coop, I smiled when I saw my grandma outside in her faded red sweater, collecting eggs into a wicker basket and scolding one of the chickens.

"You get back here right now, Martha," she said, wagging her finger at a fat red hen that seemed intent on escaping the wire fence.

Grandma looked up and noticed me then. "Well, good morning, sleepy head," she said. "High time you were out of bed. Are you on your way out? You haven't had breakfast yet."

"No, I'm just going out to talk to Grandpa for a minute," I replied. "I thought I could do with a quick walk and a bit of air. Anyway, on a morning this chilly I thought you would still be in bed too."

I didn't add another good reason for her to have slept in, that she had been up on the roof singing her heart out for at least half of the previous night.

Grandma frowned and then burst out with a hearty laugh.

"Still in bed at this time? That's a funny one, Emma. Tell your grandpa not to be late for breakfast. I had to cook two batches of eggs yesterday because he got distracted and let the first lot get cold."

"I'll tell him," I promised her. "For all the good it will do. You know what he's like when he's in the middle of something.

"Yes, that I do," Grandma admitted. "But he won't want to irk me twice in two days, mark my words, Emma."

I walked away, but I couldn't resist glancing back over my shoulder at her as I went. She was in good shape for her age. She squatted down to collect the eggs and jumped back up again like a woman of half her years. With her weather beaten skin not so much wrinkly as lived in, it was easy to forget she was over seventy.

Were her "funny turns" as Grandpa called them really any big deal? I had thought she would stop having them by now, and yet they continued. It hadn't caused any problems yet. But surely in no universe was it normal to clamber up onto the roof and sing in the middle of the night?

I spotted Grandpa in the distance and I paused to watch as he herded a stray cow back into its field. I knew he wasn't going to want to hear what I was going to say to him, but I felt like maybe I should say it all the same.

Grandpa caught sight of me and turned to wave. The cow he was herding saw her chance and lumbered back away from the gate leading into the field.

"Grandpa. The cow," I shouted, pointing. I laughed at my grandpa's expression when he saw the escapee.

He turned on his heel and firmly guided the cow back into the field again. By the time I reached him, the cow was back in the pasture and the gate was firmly closed. The big animal's chance at escape was over for another day.

"Ah, she's a wanderer that one. I should name her Emma," Grandpa said, grinning as I joined him. "She would for sure like a wander through the big city I'd be willing to bet."

I laughed. "Yes, but I'm not sure she'd know her way back when she realized that sometimes home is exactly where you need to be."

I sobered, remembering my grandma's message. "Grandma said to warn you not to be late for breakfast. She's not happy about having to redo yesterday's eggs."

He snorted. "Tell it to the cow. That old beast will be the death of me. Two days in a row she's gotten out and I still haven't worked out how she's doing it."

He shot me a sidelong glance. "But you didn't come all this way out here to warn me not to be late for breakfast. So why don't you tell me what's really on your mind?"

"Grandma had another one of her turns last night, didn't she?" I asked.

Grandpa nodded, double-checking the pasture gate. "Day four it was, so it'll be over for a time."

I said, "Grandpa, I know we haven't worried about it much before but maybe the time has finally come when Grandma needs to see a doctor. I'm sure if I asked him to, Billy would take a look at her."

Grandpa shook his head. "Don't you go gettin' ideas about telling your friends our business," he chastised.

"Grandpa, Billy's a doctor. It's not like I'm suggesting putting it all over social media."

Grandpa scrunched his nose. "Social what?"

Before I could answer, he cut me off. "Never mind. I've told you before and I'll tell you again. Your grandma's funny spells are harmless. It's not like she's going around hurtin' anyone."

"It's not normal behaviour, though," I argued. "What if she fell off the roof and got hurt? That's perfectly possible, since she's basically sleepwalking."

He chuckled. "She's not really asleep. No one could sleep through that racket, Emma. Your grandma is a beautiful woman and perfect in many ways, but her singing voice is most assuredly not one of those ways."

I said, "You're missing the point, Grandpa."

"No, Emma, you're missing the point. I'm not having no doctor coming up here poking at your grandma and upsetting her. She doesn't know about her spells. She'd be embarrassed if she knew. And I won't have you or no interfering doctor ruining that."

"But Grandpa—" I began.

"No buts. Let it go, Emma. I mean it," he declared.

"Okay," I mumbled. "You know best, Grandpa."

"Yes, I do," he said firmly.

My eyebrows shot up and he instantly looked contrite.

"Sorry. I didn't mean to be cranky. Just that I don't like people makin' a problem out of a quirk. Your grandma's what they call 'eccentric', you see. Always has been. Let's not make it into something more than that, okay?"

I nodded. "I'm sorry. I shouldn't have brought it up," I said with a shake of my head.

"Nonsense," Grandpa replied. "You can come to me with anything. You know that."

It was true. I had even told him and Grandma about the ghostly visions I had begun seeing ever since my accident back in the city, the accident that had caused me to move back to Hillbilly Hollow. Of course, I didn't often talk about what those visions involved; the idea that I was an investigator for the ghosts might have been a bit much for him and Grandma to take.

"Emma? Are you alright?" Grandpa asked.

I realized he had been talking to me while I was lost in thought. I smiled at him sheepishly.

"Sorry, Grandpa. I was a million miles away. What did you say?"

"I asked if you'd seen the weather report," he said as we started walking toward the house.

"Oh yes, I did. A light dusting of snow is on the way." I smiled, unable to contain my excitement. I had loved the snow since I was a little girl and Christmas was the absolute best time for it.

"It'll be perfect for the Christmas Garden Fair," I added.

Grandpa shook his head. "There'll be more than a light dusting. You mark my words, Emma."

I smiled as I heard a familiar bleating sound. Snowball, the little white goat that had attached herself to me ever since I came back to the farm earlier in the year, ran towards me.

Grandpa laughed. "Oh, you're in trouble, sneaking out to talk to me and leaving her behind."

"It sure looks that way," I agreed.

Snowball reached me and gently butted her head against my legs until I gave up trying to walk for a minute and reached out to scratch her behind the ears. Her bleating turned into a sound that was more like a purr.

"It looks like I'm forgiven," I said.

I managed to get Snowball out of my path and I half ran a few steps to catch back up to Grandpa. Snowball trotted happily along beside me.

As we reached the farmhouse, my stomach rumbled at the delicious smell of frying bacon and freshly cooked eggs that wafted out the door. I hadn't realized how hungry I was until that moment. I hurried inside and poured out three steaming mugs of coffee, while Grandpa washed his hands and Grandma put our breakfast onto plates.

I was reminded once more of my grandparents getting older when my grandpa's back gave a loud cracking sound as he sat down. I made a decision then.

I sat down at the table and tucked into my breakfast, waiting for the right moment to tell them my new plan.

"Oh, this is delicious, Grandma," I moaned between bites.

Grandma smiled, glowing beneath the praise.

"Are you heading on up to the fair today?" she asked me.

The Christmas Garden Fair, the town's annual Christmas event, would take place in Hollow Heights, Hillbilly Hollow's largest park. It would run for two whole weeks, clear up to Christmas and a little after. With the local historical society I was a member of on hold over the colder months, I'd needed something to do around the community. So I'd volunteered to help out with the fair. I'd been going up to the park every day for the last couple weeks, helping to hang lights and hand out flyers.

"Yes, I'm going to the park today if you don't need me here for anything," I said. Then I added, "I actually wanted to talk to you both about that."

I saw Grandpa give a slight shake of his head, signalling me when Grandma wasn't looking, but I ignored it. Now would be as good a time as any to bring up what was on my mind.

Grandma said, "If it's anything to do with the fair then don't worry. We can take care of your chores around here for the next two weeks, can't we, Ed?"

Grandpa nodded enthusiastically, still giving me a

warning look.

I said, "Well, that's the thing. I was actually going to let Mrs. Schneider know I'm dropping out. There's so much that needs doing around the farm, especially with the snow coming soon. And it doesn't seem fair that I go off and do something fun and leave all of that to you two."

Grandma said, "Nonsense, we enjoy the farm work. And you didn't come back here to be our servant, Emma. Go up there and enjoy it. You deserve it after all the work you've put into getting the Christmas Garden set up."

I shook my head, but Grandma was having none of it.

Grandpa sat in silence, sipping his coffee.

"There's more to it than you're saying, Emma," Grandma guessed. "I can tell by your face. So why don't you just spit it out?"

"Well," I started.

I felt Grandpa's eyes burning into the side of my head and I glanced at him. His look said it all.

I cleared my throat and suddenly decided I couldn't go against Grandpa's wishes. I couldn't tell Grandma about her funny spells, if he didn't think it was good for her to know. I had to say something, though.

"I don't mean to be rude, Grandma. But you and Grandpa aren't getting any younger, and I just think it would be good for you both to have a little more time to take it easy, especially now that the colder months are here."

Grandma laughed. "She's calling us old, Ed."

"Yes, I got that. Quite somethin' coming from a grand-daughter I can run rings around." He laughed.

He had a fair point there. Even after the time I had spent back on the farm, he could still outwork me without even breaking a sweat. I had gotten fitter, toned up a bit, there was no denying that, but I was still a long way from being as tough as either of my grandparents. That was what city living had done to me, I guessed. It had made me soft.

"You know, Dorothy, she does have a point about one thing," Grandpa said with a twinkle in his eye. "I reckon these days you and I might be a bit past splitting wood and firing up the wood burning stove in the mornings."

Grandma pretended to think about it. "You know something, Ed? I reckon you're right. She can take care of that for us and then still do the Christmas Garden Fair."

Grandma thought we'd found a compromise, a way to make me feel useful and still get to do the fair. She didn't know my grandpa hated the wood chopping and the stove. He had just taken the opportunity to palm off the most hated job on the farm to me.

He turned to me now, his face a picture of innocence.

"What do you say, Emma? Is that a fair compromise?"

I wanted to say no, but I felt myself nodding.

"Yes. Yes, it is," I said, forcing a smile.

Grandpa winked at me when Grandma got up to start clearing away the breakfast pots. That wink said it all. I had been well and truly played.

My cell phone started ringing before Grandpa could gloat too much. I glanced at the screen, expecting to see Suzy's name or maybe even Billy's. Instead, it was an out of town number. I picked up the phone and stood quickly.

"I'm sorry, I have to take this. Grandma, leave those pots and I'll take care of them when I'm done."

"You're a good kid, Emma," she said as she sat down with her cup of coffee.

I hurried out of the kitchen and went to stand in the yard. Snowball immediately trotted out behind me, no doubt afraid she would be left out of another trip around the farm. She was going to be disappointed.

I took the call.

"Emma Hooper," I said into the phone.

"Emma? Hi. Eva Baron here from Baron's Construction. I found your contact info on a freelance site where you're listed as a graphic designer. I wondered if maybe you had some time to fit in a small job for me?"

"Sure. What exactly are you looking for?" I asked.

She talked a little about the company and the story she wanted to tell through her branding. She told me that the company needed a full rebranding and she wanted me to design their new logo, their website header and a glossy flyer. I almost whooped with excitement. A new work project was exactly what I needed.

"I can definitely help you with that. My email address is Emma dot Hooper, all lower case, at Emma Hooper Designs dot com. If you could send over your requirements, your brand colors and a link to your website so I can get a feel for the sort of thing that would match your brand well, I can get you a quote within forty-eight hours."

"Perfect," Eva said. "I look forward to hearing from you, Emma."

She hung up before I had a chance to say goodbye. It almost made me nostalgic for New York, where everyone was always rushing around, too busy even to say goodbye on a call. The nostalgia didn't last long before Snowball bleated and rubbed herself against my legs, almost as though she knew I was thinking about my old life.

"Ah, I'm not going anywhere girl," I whispered as I headed back into the house. It was true. A recent visit back to New York to solve the murder of my old landlady had reminded me that Hillbilly Hollow was my true home now.

"Good news?" Grandpa asked as I walked over to the sink and began to fill it with hot water.

"Yes, actually." I smiled. "I've just landed a new client, assuming she's happy with my quote."

"You do too much, Emma," my grandma chastised me.

I rolled my eyes and said, "Coming from the woman who runs a farm, belongs to a quilting circle, and is talking about joining a book club. Not to mention all the community events you participate in."

"But those are fun things, Emma."

"So is this to me. I love graphic design. It's the one thing I'm actually good at."

"Nonsense. You're good at more than just that," Grandpa said. He winked at me again. "You're going to make an excellent wood cutter."

I groaned inwardly but on the outside I just laughed. "You know something, Grandpa? I think you might just be right about that."

I finished washing and drying the dishes. Three times I tripped over Snowball as I put the dishes back away.

"You're definitely at least half dog," I said to her as she looked up at me with her baleful brown eyes. "Don't worry. I love dogs too."

By the time I was all finished with the pots, my grandparents were back outdoors and I had to go looking for my grandpa. I found him tending to some empty land.

"Just turning it over to stop the frost from ruining good soil," he explained when he saw my confused look.

"If you don't need my help, I was going to head out to the park and just double check everything is in order for the opening," I said. "Do you know what happened to the keys to the truck?"

"Oh, it's the big opening tomorrow, isn't it? You've all worked so hard and I'm sure this year's Christmas Garden will be the best one yet. But I get why you feel like you have to check everything one last time. The keys are in the drawer. Take as long as you like, Emma. We've got the farm under control."

"Thanks." I beamed.

I went back into the house and found the keys to the truck.

"Sorry, Snowball, this one's going to be a solo mission I'm afraid," I said as I scratched the goat's ears once more.

I ducked out quickly, making sure she couldn't escape out into the front yard as I went. I got into the battered old truck, the very one I had learned to drive in, and headed towards Hollow Heights Park.

I knew Grandpa was right; we'd all put a lot of work into the Christmas Garden Fair and it was going to be perfect. But he was also right about me just needing to check it one more time. As paranoid as that probably made me, I was a perfectionist, and I would rather encounter any issues today while there was still time to put them right than find them tomorrow and ruin the big opening.

I WENT into town and spent the rest of the day at the park, working with other volunteers to string a few more colorful lights from the trees and put the finishing touches on the decorative Christmas displays. By the end of the day's work, I was confident we had got everything done to perfection. The Christmas fair was as ready as we could make it.

I couldn't help feeling proud of my efforts, as I glimpsed the twinkling lights in my rear-view mirror while driving away from Hollow Heights. I would head home and get a little sleep and be all ready for the opening tomorrow.

2

I straightened up and pressed on the small of my back until it gave a satisfying cracking sound. The crack did little to ease the burning in my muscles, though. My back hurt and my arms were even worse. And I had only split and carried in half of the wood for the wood burning stove. I'd been working beneath the cold glow of a bare bulb from the woodshed, because it wasn't yet light outside.

I stifled a yawn as I put down the splitter, grabbed an armful of wood, and headed back past the outhouse, carrying in the next load. Snowball trotted merrily alongside me. Her joyful, almost skipping gait made me shake my head in wonder. Didn't she know it was only four o'clock in the morning? Morning? Ha. That was a joke. It was the middle of the night as far as I was concerned.

That was the main trouble with this job. Not the endless chopping or the fight to get the flame going. No, the worst part was the early start. Until the wood burner kicked in, the whole house was freezing, so whoever was doing that job had to be the first one up. I vowed to myself I would split the wood for tomorrow tonight and at least get an extra hour in bed the next morning.

"Do you think I'll stick to that, Snowball?" I asked her as I struggled in with the wood.

She gave me a look that was almost a smile.

I laughed. "Yeah, that's what I thought too," I said to her.

An hour later, the wood was all split and lugged inside. The logs were arranged in the stove exactly how I'd seen Grandpa do them. The biggest, thickest logs were on the bottom of the pile, working up to the smaller ones at the top. The tiny pieces of kindling were scattered over those and, in theory, the flames should have been taking. But they weren't.

I pulled my fingers back and yelped when the extra long match burned down too far, scorching my fingers for the third time.

"Having some trouble with that, dear?" my grandma's voice asked from behind me.

I hadn't heard her come in and I jumped. Then I felt my cheeks burn with embarrassment when I realized how pathetic my fire-lighting attempts must look to an old hand like Grandma.

"Yes, a little trouble," I replied.

"No matter. Here's a little trick that might help. Just don't let your grandpa catch you cheating," she said with a wink.

She went to a drawer in the kitchen and pulled out a newspaper. She tore off a few sheets and balled them up, before bringing them back. She laid the crumpled papers carefully on the top of the pile of wood and held a match to them. They took instantly and passed the flames on to the kindling.

"So, that's the secret," I said with a laugh.

"It's my secret. But your grandpa has his own natural

knack for fire-starting. He would never approve of my little 'cheat'."

Within ten minutes, the fire was burning merrily away and the kitchen was more than pleasantly warm. Grandma slipped her coat on.

"Where are you going?" I asked.

Grandma laughed. "Out to get the eggs. Where did you think I was going?"

"I didn't realize it had gotten so late in the morning," I admitted.

I stood up and followed Grandma. By the time we had collected all of the eggs and fed the chickens, Grandpa was out in one of the fields somewhere. Grandma and I went back inside and Grandma started making a batter.

"I thought we might have pancakes today for ..." She trailed off and came back with a shout. "Stop it, girl! You put that down!"

I couldn't help but laugh at Snowball's total disregard for the instruction. She continued to happily munch her way through Grandma's tea towel.

Grandma tutted to herself and went to fetch another one. She left it high up on the counter out of Snowball's reach.

"I swear that goat costs us more in tea towels than your Grandpa does in shirts," she said.

The back door opened and Grandpa came in.

"Did I hear my name taken in vain in here?" he asked with a pretend scowl.

"Oh, always." Grandma laughed.

We ate the delicious pancakes covered in maple syrup. I looked at my watch after breakfast was over. I still had a couple hours to kill before I had to be at the park. I debated going back to bed, but it didn't feel quite right going to bed while my grandparents worked. I decided instead to go into town and call in at Suzy's shop to catch up with her. Ever since she and Brian got back from their honeymoon months ago I hadn't seen as much of my best friend as I used to.

"If you don't need me, I was thinking of dropping in on Suzy before I head over to the park," I said as I put the last of the dishes away.

"Fine with me," Grandpa said. "You know you don't have to ask. The truck is out front whenever you need it."

"Thanks," I said.

I kissed his cheek and then Grandma's.

"Enjoy the fair, honey. And say hi to Suzy for me," Grandma called to my back as I hurried away.

"I will," I promised.

I DROVE over to Suzy's place, getting lucky and grabbing a parking space right out in front of the shop. I could feel the chill in the wind even through my winter coat and I hurried into the warmth of the shop. As I rushed in, a customer came out, leaving the store empty, except for Suzy and her racks of clothes.

"Morning, Emma," my friend greeted me cheerfully as I hopped up to sit on the counter by the register. "Want a donut?"

She reached under the counter and produced a donut box that was half empty.

"No thanks, I already had breakfast," I said, peering into the crumb-littered box. "But what happened here? These donuts look like they were attacked by a pack of ravenous dinosaurs."

"Very funny." Suzy stuck out her bottom lip in a mock

pout, as she hopped up onto the counter beside me. "If you must know, I was a little hungry this morning."

"A little hungry? A T-Rex couldn't eat that many donuts."

Suzy wrinkled her nose and shook out her blond curls. "Moving on..."

I took the hint. "My grandpa reckons the forecast for the snow is wrong," I said, changing the subject. "He said there won't just be flurries; there'll be a full on snow storm."

"Your grandpa's right," Suzy replied knowingly.

I raised an eyebrow and she laughed.

"Okay, I have no idea if it will happen or not," she admitted. "But if Ed predicts it, I'm inclined to believe it. I wonder how bad the extra snow in the Christmas Garden will annoy Betty Blackwell?"

"What do you mean? What does Betty Blackwell have to do with the Christmas Garden?" I asked, sure I must have missed something, judging by the way Suzy was looking at me, waiting for my reaction.

"You haven't heard, have you? I thought you'd come here to moan about it. Do you live under a rock or something, Emma?"

"No, I just tune out the town gossip. I know I can rely on you to give me the highlight reel," I replied.

"Well then, how's this for a highlight? It seems you're not the only one with too much time on her hands now that the old fort is closed for the winter and the historical society has nothing to do."

Suzy was referring to the old nineteenth century fort on the edge of town, where I often volunteered to participate in old fort days, entertaining visitors during the warm months. The fort was run by the local historical society, of which Betty Blackwell was president.

Suzy continued. "Betty Blackwell has just gone and got

herself put in charge of organising the volunteers at the Christmas Garden Fair."

"Ugh," I groaned. "You mean to tell me I'm going to have to answer to her from now on? She's such a nitpicker, and she can't get along with anyone."

"Being stern and abrupt is just her way, Emma. She should have been a school teacher."

I snorted. "I don't think many kids would have enjoyed that school."

"No, probably not," Suzy conceded.

"So, how did she do it? Coming in on the fair management after all the actual setting up was done? Getting to boss everyone around and not do any real work?"

Suzy shrugged. "Mrs. Schneider and her go back years, don't they? And Mrs. Schneider's arthritis is playing up in the cold. So Betty saw her chance and took it."

My cell phone buzzed in my pocket and I had a horrible feeling it was going to be Betty calling to tell me I was late to the park, or that I lacked dedication, or one of the hundreds of other things she had said to me over my time with the historical society.

It wasn't Betty. It was a text message from Billy. I slipped my phone back away hoping Suzy would let it go. She didn't, of course.

"Not answering a text. That's not like you at all. And that half smile you're trying to hide means it was from Billy, wasn't it?" Suzy grinned.

I sighed and nodded.

"So answer him," she said.

"I will when I'm back in the truck," I said.

She rolled her eyes. "Why don't you just date him already?"

"Because it's not like that, Suzy. We're friends, that's all."

"Yeah right. That's not what he wants and we both know it."

I didn't bother trying to deny it. I knew Suzy was right, but it was easier to tell myself neither of us wanted more, because I really did care a lot about Billy and I didn't want to hurt him.

"Seriously, Emma. Why don't you give him a chance? He's sweet, good looking, you actually care about him. What's he missing?"

"He isn't missing anything. It's just ... it's complicated that's all."

"Complicated my foot. You just don't want to commit to dating him because you're afraid if it doesn't work out, that'll be the end of your friendship."

I frowned. "You know me far too well," I said.

She grinned. "Yup. Now you'd best get going or you're gonna be late and Betty won't like that. She'll probably put you on toilet cleaning duty or something."

I shuddered at the thought. "Yeah, you're right. See you later," I said, sliding down from the counter and making my way to the door.

"Give Billy a chance," Suzy shouted after me.

I just waved in reply. Suzy was still laughing as the door closed behind me. I hurried back to my truck and pulled my cell phone out again. I found myself a little too eager to read the message.

The text message was short and to the point.

BILLY: Lunch?

I SMILED to myself and then shook my head as if to clear it. I wasn't going to go down the road of asking myself what it meant that I was always so happy to hear from him. Anyway, it wasn't like I could say yes to this invite.

ME: Sorry, can't. It's the first day of the Christmas Garden.

I PAUSED for a second and added a sad emoji before pressing send. I'd barely gotten the truck's engine going when my phone buzzed again.

BILLY: I'll come to U. See U around two.

I COULDN'T STOP the smile from spreading across my face this time, and I didn't attempt to wipe it away. Instead, I pulled away from the parking spot, telling myself I was just happy at the thought of seeing a friend. And having someone to vent to if Betty Blackwell wound up being her usual charming self.

When I pulled up into the parking lot at Hollow Heights Park, the area was still almost empty. We had an hour or so before the Christmas Garden's grand opening, which was in reality no grander than the clock striking eleven am and old Marty Flint, the groundskeeper, pushing open the gate to that section of the park.

I quickly typed out a response to Billy, telling him I would look forward to seeing him, and then I stuffed my phone back into my pocket and headed towards the makeshift tent that was being used as the fair's headquarters.

I wasn't even halfway there when I heard the raised voice of Betty Blackwell rolling across the gardens. Shouting already. A moment later, I saw Frank Clarkson, who looked after the reindeer in the temporary petting zoo, stomping out of the tent, his face red with anger.

"Don't you dare walk away from me, Frank Clarkson!" Betty shouted, following him out of the tent.

"I'm most certainly not goin' to stay here to be insulted by you," he replied. "You've barely been here ten minutes and already you think you're in charge."

Frank's usually red face was an especially bright shade today, his thick gray eyebrows climbing so high into his wrinkled forehead that they nearly met his hairline

"I'm in charge of this event," Betty reminded him. "And it would do you well to remember that."

Frank scrunched up his scruffy face which, judging by its stubble, hadn't been shaved in a couple weeks. "Sounds about right. Turning up once the hard part is done and taking credit for everyone else's work."

Betty flushed pink and her mouth gaped open and closed like a fish out of water.

It was pretty much the same thing Suzy and I had said, but to speak to Betty that way to her face seemed more than a little harsh, I thought. As abrupt as Betty was, her heart was in the right place and she was always volunteering for community stuff around the town. The more cynical town's folk said it was because she loved having power over people, no matter how irrelevant that power might be. Personally, I liked to think it was because she was lonely or wanted the best for the town.

Frank was headed straight for me, storming in the direction of the reindeer pen.

"This isn't over, Frank!" Betty shouted after him.

He didn't even bother to reply.

"That woman will be the death of me," he muttered as he passed me.

Not wanting to get involved in the argument, I pretended not to hear him and kept walking towards Betty. She spotted me and disappeared back into the tent. She came straight out again before I could reach her, a clipboard and pen clutched in her hand.

It occurred to me that the older woman, with her tightly pulled back hair and high-collared blouses, was rarely seen without a clipboard. It seemed to add to her air of authority.

"Emma, how nice of you to join us," she greeted me, looking pointedly at her watch.

I chose to ignore the sarcasm and smiled at her.

"Glad to be here, Betty. It's always good to do our bit, right? I see Frank is giving you some trouble."

Betty just made a humph sound.

I wanted to ask her what their argument had been about, but I knew she wouldn't tell me. Anyway, I reminded myself that I didn't want to get involved.

"Some of the lights in the patch of trees behind the apple cider stand were pulled down last night. I need you to restring them," said Betty.

I nodded, bristling inside at her lack of a "please". It didn't much matter, though. I would have fixed the lights anyway. Too much hard work had gone into this to leave a patch of trees unlit.

"Any idea who vandalized the lights?" I asked.

Betty shook her head. "No. It'll be teenagers, I'm sure. You know what they're like. Too much time on their hands. If they were my kids, I'd soon find something for them to do and stop them from going around terrorizing people."

"I'll get right to work repairing the display," I said,

avoiding the subject. While I was annoyed about the lights, it was a stretch to say that the local teens terrorized people.

I moved away from Betty and found Colin, the handyman, and begged a set of ladders off him. Then I went to get a new string of lights. I soon managed to get them all hung and switched on just in time for the Christmas Garden to open.

I hadn't realized how many families with small children had begun gathering at the gate, until they began making their way inside. It was worth every minute of the time I'd given to repairing the display when I heard the children gasping with amazement and saw them pointing and smiling, their cheeks pink from the cold and their eyes glittering with excitement.

The Christmas Garden was pretty spectacular, even if I was a little biased. All of the trees were strung with lights, and the side of the sports centre had been decorated with a large snow scene complete with Santa and all of his reindeer, courtesy of a local artist.

All of the refreshment and game stalls were decked out with more lights and the air was full of the scents of apple cider, eggnog and hot cocoa. Mixed with the smell of frying meat and onions, it was enough to make anyone hungry. I realized my stomach was rumbling.

It wouldn't be long until Billy came for lunch, so I decided not to ruin it by grabbing a hotdog. Instead, I opted for a cup of hot cocoa to keep my hands warm as I sold tickets for the synthetic ice skating rink.

The air was soon full of children laughing and screaming as they chased each other around the rink. I couldn't help but smile. It was scenes like this one that made me glad I'd come back to Hillbilly Hollow.

"Excuse me, miss. Would you be able to recommend a nice spot for lunch?" Billy's voice came from behind me.

I turned and he grinned at me. He clutched a paper bag from which drifted a smell so delicious that it was all I could do not to take it from him and start eating right there.

"I think I can manage that." I smiled. "Just give me a minute to let Maggie know I'm taking a break."

I walked away from him, feeling his eyes on my back. I found Maggie, another volunteer, on the other side of the rink, where she was helping kids choose their skates.

"Maggie, I'm going to take a quick break for lunch. Are you okay on your own for a bit?" I asked.

Maggie smiled and nodded her head of thick red hair.

"Sure. Take as long as you like. It's quiet yet. It won't get really busy until the schools let out. Right now we've only got the littler kids."

I thanked her and hurried back to Billy. I beckoned him to follow me and led him to the truck in the parking lot. I clambered in and took my gloves off, instantly feeling the cold biting into my fingers. I switched the heater on. Billy climbed in beside me. Our breath made white plumes in the air, but the heater soon took care of that.

"Not exactly picturesque, is it?" Billy asked with a grin, handing me a huge hotdog and a carton of fries.

I bit into the hotdog and moaned. "Oh wow, that's so good," I said. "And this may not be picturesque, but it's warm. And the company is good."

"That it is," he replied.

I took a moment to work on my hotdog.

"You know Betty Blackwell has managed to get herself put in charge of the fair?" I said when my hotdog was almost gone and I felt a bit fuller.

"I didn't, but I can well imagine it," Billy replied. "How many people has she upset so far?"

"Just one that I know of, but it's early days yet." I laughed.

"You know, this is just like old times. Sitting in your grandpa's truck, eating carnival food and watching the world go by," Billy said. "I've said it a lot these past few months, but it's great to have you back, Emma. I'm almost glad that taxi hit you back in the city and sent you home to Hillbilly Hollow to recuperate. If that hadn't happened, I guess you'd still be living a busy life in New York, forgetting all about us hicks back home."

I laughed, but felt awkward, the way I always did when Billy talked too much about how good it was to have me back. Anyway, where did this come from? How did we go from giggling at bossy Betty to being back here, at the place we skirted where Billy let me know Suzy was right and he wanted more, and I wriggled my way out of it, careful not to hurt his feelings more than I had to.

I couldn't think of any way to change the subject, so I just nodded and bit into my remaining hotdog and looked out the window while I finished eating.

3

After finishing lunch with Billy, I walked across the park again towards the skating rink.

"I'm back, Maggie," I said as I arrived at the edge of the fake ice.

Maggie's green eyes darted left and right like she expected to be attacked by some unseen enemy at any moment.

"You need to sneak away through those trees and then come back again across the main square," she said.

"Huh? Why?" I asked.

Maggie smiled sheepishly. "Betty came over here just after you left for lunch, demanding to know where you were. I figured Betty probably doesn't believe in taking breaks. So I panicked and told her you'd gone to do a last minute walk through of the lights before things got too busy."

That made sense. Maggie was indeed expecting an attack at any moment. A Betty Blackwell style tongue lashing.

"Got it," I said. "Thanks for covering for me."

"Any time. We're the ones who did all of the hard work, so I reckon we deserve a lunch break," she said with a laugh.

I sneaked around into the trees, feeling like some sort of spy. It was kind of exciting, ducking down whenever I heard voices. Once I was in the thick of the trees, I straightened up and walked tall. It wouldn't matter if I was seen here. This was where I was meant to be. It wasn't as much fun now that it wasn't a covert mission, so I hurried back to the edge of the trees and got ready to step out into the square.

But then a flash of movement caught my eye near the sports center. I paused, trying to work out what was going on. A woman in a green coat, the hood pulled up to cover her hair, stood with her back to me in front of the Christmas mural. At first glance, she looked like she was just looking at scene, enjoying the colors, and maybe smiling at Rudolph's red nose. But the strange way her elbow moved up and down and the way she glanced furtively from side to side told me she was up to something weird.

I waited and watched. She took a step back to admire her handiwork and I saw what had been going on. A large square of the mural had been spray painted black. The woman in the green coat tossed a spray paint can to the ground and began to hurriedly walk away.

I was frozen for a moment, so shocked that someone would vandalize the mural that I almost let her get away. Then I came to my senses.

"Hey," I shouted as I stepped out from among the trees. "What do you think you're doing?"

4

The woman didn't glance back. She didn't have to look at me to know that I had to be talking to her. She started to run and I ran after her. I wasn't exactly in shape, but all of the work on the farm had gotten rid of the few stubborn extra pounds city life had given me and I wasn't a total slouch. I was no Olympic gold medallist, but I knew I could hold my own, and I was confident I could catch her.

I was starting to gain on the woman, my eyes glued to her green coat so I wouldn't lose sight of her in the thin crowd, when a shout went up behind me.

"Emma, catch him!"

Catch *him*? Who was shouting and couldn't they see it was a woman I was chasing?

I risked a glance back over my shoulder and what I saw stopped me in my tracks. I knew I would have to give up my pursuit of the green-coated woman, because suddenly a new problem had presented itself. Five of the six reindeer from the petting zoo were darting around the main square.

The sixth and final one was heading straight for me—the *him* that I was evidently expected to catch.

My mouth dropped open at sight of the chaos the animals were creating. People were running from them, shrieking. It was unnecessary – reindeer were lovely, gentle creatures –but the panic was starting to infect them too and they ran this way and that. It would have been comical if it wasn't for the fact that the reindeer could end up getting hurt if the crowd continued to frighten them. Park volunteers, like the middle-aged man nearby who had shouted at me, were attempting to round up the deer.

The animal heading my way was coming straight for me. His head was down and he was fixed on his course.

"Easy boy," I called to him.

If he heard me, my words had no effect on the beast whatsoever. He just kept coming. If I didn't move, I knew I would be mowed down. The deer just wanted to get away from the chaos behind him and he had spotted a clear path to freedom. Except for me blocking the way.

I moved to the side slightly and raised my arms in front of me, ready to make a grab for the creature. I tensed, waiting for the right moment.

"It's okay," I told the deer in what I hoped was a soothing tone. "Everything's going to be just fine. No one is going to hurt you."

The reindeer was almost to me when I leapt forward, arms outstretched. I flew through the air and came to land face down in the mud. The reindeer rushed straight past me and I could have sworn he was laughing as he ran away.

Humiliated by my failed attempt to be a reindeer whisperer, I got to my feet. I glanced down at my front and knew that no amount of brushing at the mud on my coat would get rid of it. I attempted to wipe the worst away, but it was no use. All I was doing was smearing the mud around.

Shouts of alarm and small childrens' whoops of joy filled the air as one of the reindeer crashed into a nearby apple cider stand. The board structure collapsed and a huge vat of apple cider spilled onto the ground. The air was instantly filled with the scent of its sweetness.

At least Mollie Garrow, the volunteer who had been manning the stall, was able to catch hold of the reindeer who had careened into the stand. I watched as she rubbed his neck and whispered to him. Within seconds, he was his usual calm self again.

Okay, I thought to myself, I get it now. Grab them and then try to calm them down, rather than the other way around.

With one reindeer captured, that still left five on the loose and I headed closer to try and help catch them. Colin, Marty, and Marty's son David had one of the deer cornered near the tennis court, but it seemed like they were all afraid to grab it. I decided to start there. I had learned from Mollie and was confident I could calm the creature now that he was cornered.

I headed for the small group and, as I hurried that way, I wondered how the reindeer had gotten out in the first place. They'd never managed to escape before. Maybe they'd had lessons from one of Grandpa's cows or Grandma's chickens, I thought with a smile.

Then it occurred to me that there was a more plausible explanation. The woman in the green coat could have opened the gate to their pen, before proceeding to deface the mural. She must have known the escape of the deer would cause chaos and maybe she figured she could do her sneaky deed and then slip away unseen as we all chased after the reindeer.

It had almost worked, too. If I hadn't sneaked through the wooded area to avoid Betty Blackwell, no one would have seen what had been done to the mural until the culprit was long gone. By the time the damage was noticed, none of us would have had the tiniest inkling who was behind the act.

But I pushed thoughts of the green-coated woman aside. I would figure out a way to deal with her later. For now, there was a more pressing job in front of me.

A couple more of the reindeer had been brought under control by the time I reached Colin, Marty, and David. They were still ranged around their trapped reindeer, which was snorting with annoyance, sending plumes of white into the air. The beast's eyes rolled in their sockets as he desperately looked for a means of escape.

"You're not afraid of him are you?" I asked the fellows with a soft laugh.

"Looks like *you* should be," Marty said, grinning pointedly down at the mud caked over my coat.

I felt myself blush slightly at the evidence of my clumsiness. "Seems these critters are a little trickier than I gave them credit for," I admitted. "They're harmless, though. Watch."

I stepped between the three men and slowly approached the reindeer.

"Hey, little guy. How did you get out, huh?" I asked quietly as I approached the animal. I had seen my grandpa creep up to nervous calves often enough to know how it was done.

The deer watched me closely. His big brown eyes reminded me of Snowball's eyes and that made me more confident that I was right to call him harmless. I reached out a hand and gently stroked his velvety nose. He pulled away a little.

"It's okay," I whispered. "It's okay. Everything's just fine now."

He relaxed at my soft touch and the sound of my voice, and within seconds, he was nuzzling his face against my hand, licking my palm with his wet tongue.

"He's looking for a treat," David said, laughing.

"Let's get you back into your pen," I said to the reindeer. "I don't know where your handler is, but I'll bet he's worried about where you've got off to."

I turned to the men.

"Do you think you three can get him back now you've seen he isn't a ferocious beast? Frank Clarkson can take over once you lead the deer to the pen. I'll go and help clean up the mess from the apple cider stand."

Colin nodded sheepishly. "Sure. Thanks Emma," he said.

I nodded to him and started to make my way towards the broken cider stand. Most of the crowd had dispersed now and only a few onlookers remained. The staff were scattered, still trying to catch the last of the reindeer on the loose.

I was halfway between Colin and the others and the apple cider stand when a long, shrill scream pierced the air.

The sound made me freeze in my tracks, the hairs on the back of my neck standing up. It hadn't been a scream of joy, or even the scream of someone ending up face down in the mud like I had.

It was the scream of someone utterly terrified.

5

The noise was coming from the direction of the reindeer pen. I didn't think, I just acted. I took off in the direction of the pen as fast as my legs would carry me. Much faster than I had been when I was chasing the woman in the green coat. That scream had a sense of urgency about it that made sprinting the only option.

I reached the reindeer pen to find Betty Blackwell standing alone in the centre of the enclosure, her face pasty white and her bottom lip quivering. She was pointing down at something I couldn't see because the fence blocked my view.

Not until I rounded the corner of the fence and entered through the open gate did I see what was lying on the ground at Betty's feet. It was something much worse than I could have imagined.

It was the motionless body of Frank Clarkson.

I was no expert, but I got the immediate impression the reindeer handler was dead.

For a moment I froze where I was, stunned at the sight of the still body lying prone across the dirt. But then, I felt a strange sense of calm wash over me. I had dealt with death before, although generally on the investigative end.

I crossed the pen and touched Betty's arm. Someone had to take charge here. Right now, Betty obviously wasn't in the right frame of mind to do it.

"What happened?" I asked.

My touch broke Betty from her stunned trance and she shook her head.

"I-I don't know. I found him...like this." She nodded toward Frank. "It looks like he banged his head."

It looked more like someone else had banged his head for him, I thought. The dead man lay sprawled on the straw-strewn ground, a red-stained gash on the back of his skull standing out starkly against his thin gray hair. His limbs were bent at an awkward angle, positioned exactly as they must have been when he'd fallen, as if he had been killed instantly.

My mind jumped all over the place, as I tried to make sense of it. I'd spent so much time in recent months solving mysteries that I seemed to click into amateur detective mode automatically now, when confronted with violence.

Who could have been responsible for this? Betty? No, surely not. Surely she wouldn't have drawn attention to herself this way if she'd killed Frank. Or maybe she would. Maybe being the one to find him would give her the perfect cover and ensure she wasn't even a suspect.

I shook aside the questions, realizing I needed to focus on the most important things first.

"Someone call an ambulance—and Sheriff Tucker," I shouted to the few people who had heard Betty's scream and wandered over to the pen. "And find somewhere else secure to put the reindeer. They can't be here. This is a crime scene now."

I was surprised at how strong and confident my voice sounded, and I was even more surprised when onlookers jumped into action and began to follow my orders.

"I'll make the call. You find somewhere else for the reindeer, and we'll get them herded over there," I heard Marty telling someone.

I turned back to Betty. "Betty, are you alright? Would you like a glass of brandy? I can ask someone to go and get you one."

"Certainly not, it's the middle of the afternoon," Betty snapped. "Now we'd better get this area sectioned off before guests make their way over and see this... unpleasantness. It presents a terrible impression of the Christmas Garden."

I raised my eyebrows. It seemed Betty was back to her usual charming self.

6

T he captured reindeer had all been taken to
another pen and secured inside by Marty and the
others. There were very few people left at the
Christmas Garden. The escaped reindeer had cleared out
the majority of them and of the stragglers that remained, it
seemed most of them just wanted a peek at poor Frank.

Betty had taken charge of the pen containing Frank's
body. She stood in front of it, far enough away that no one
approaching her would see more than the fence. Any time
someone approached her, she turned them away with her
cutting tongue and off they went with their tails between
their legs.

It was good to see her so quickly recovered from the
shock of finding the victim, but it niggled at the edge of my
mind. I couldn't help but wonder why she wasn't more
shaken up. I felt pretty shaken myself and I wasn't even the
one who found him.

I told myself everyone had their own way of coping with
tragedy, and that Betty's method was clearly working for her.

I was pulled back out of my thoughts when a young woman holding the hand of a little girl approached Betty. The child was excited, bouncing up and down as she walked, her mouth moving quickly as she chattered away. Her mom smiled down at her.

"Nothing to see here, Mrs. Abernathy. Move on back to the main square please," Betty told the woman as they approached. Betty angled her body so that the mother and child couldn't get close enough to see the grisly scene inside the pen.

Her no-nonsense tone did nothing to quell the girl's excitement, but it did get the attention of her mom. Mrs. Abernathy focused on Betty and offered a friendly smile.

"I'm sorry. Are we in the wrong place? Isn't this where we get tickets to see Santa?"

"No, it most certainly is not," Betty snapped. She softened her tone slightly when it evidently occurred to her that Mrs. Abernathy most likely wasn't bringing her daughter to see a dead body. "Santa will be here later, and tickets are available from the ice rink."

"Thank you," Mrs. Abernathy replied. She smiled down at her daughter. "Why don't we go and get a candy apple and then we can see Santa, okay? He's not here yet. He must be busy with all of his elves."

Mrs. Abernathy tried to lead the child away, but the little girl dug her heels in.

"But Mommy, she's lying," the little girl said in a voice loud enough to make her mom blush.

Betty frowned. "I beg your pardon?" she said to the girl.

The girl, unfazed by the icy tone from Betty, crossed her arms.

"I saw Santa in the parking lot," she said. "I asked why

he wasn't in his sleigh and he said the reindeer are resting so they're ready for Christmas Eve."

"Listen honey," Mrs. Abernathy said. "He's still getting ready. He'll have to check his good and naughty list so he knows who to give the best presents to, okay?"

This seemed to appease the child slightly and she allowed herself to be led away. They'd only gone a few steps before Betty called out.

"Mrs. Abernathy, wait," she said.

It sounded more like an order than a polite request and I found myself stepping closer, just in case Mrs. Abernathy didn't respond kindly to the tone. I couldn't stand by and allow Betty to ruin this child's day.

Mrs. Abernathy turned back to Betty but she didn't look angry. She was obviously used to Betty Blackwell's commanding ways.

"What is it?" she asked.

"Did you really see Santa in the parking lot?" Betty demanded.

Mrs. Abernathy nodded and Betty turned to me, looking furious. "Why is he here so early? Did you do this?"

I was startled. "No, I didn't. If I remember correctly, Santa wasn't meant to be here until the weekend. It was your idea to change that and have him come every day. And you said no one but you could be trusted to organize it properly."

I was saved from Betty's cutting response by the little Abernathy girl.

"Look! I told you he was here now," she said, pointing excitedly.

I looked where she was pointing, and sure enough, a man in a Santa suit complete with a big bushy white beard was approaching us.

"Well, this is just unacceptable," Betty griped, seemingly forgetting all about guarding the body in the reindeer pen.

She stormed off in the direction of the arriving Santa.

"I think maybe we should leave and come back tomorrow," Mrs. Abernathy said to her daughter.

She obviously wasn't aware of Frank's corpse lying not far off, but she could surely tell that something was going on here.

"But Mommy, Santa's here. And I wanted to tell him about the dolly I want," the girl replied.

I walked over to Mrs. Abernathy and the girl.

"You know something?" I asked.

The girl shook her head, looking up at me with big brown eyes.

"That's not the real Santa. The real Santa was too busy to come today. That's why Mrs. Blackwell is so upset. She doesn't want any boys and girls seeing anyone but the real Santa."

"Really?" the girl asked.

"Really," I said.

"But the real Santa is definitely coming?" she confirmed.

I nodded. "Yes. He'll be here tomorrow and every other day."

The girl turned to her mom. "Okay, we can come back later."

Mrs. Abernathy gave me a grateful look and led her daughter away.

I headed after Betty. I didn't know what was going on with this Santa, but I wanted to make sure she didn't run him off for good. I caught up to her and we walked together across the lawn towards Santa.

"I won't have him or anyone else ruining this event,"

Betty grumbled. "Frank Clarkson has already done enough damage today without this happening."

I raised my eyebrows. She made it sound as though poor old Frank had got himself killed just to spite her.

"Maybe this is the same Santa you ordered and he's just running a little early," I tried to reason with her.

"Well, he shouldn't be. He should be on time," Betty snapped. "Not that I'd expect you to know that."

I ignored the barbed comment as we met with the Santa Claus.

"I'm sorry, but you're far too early. Please leave and come back at the time you were requested to be here," Betty greeted him.

The Santa's eyes darted left and then right, as if checking to see if the coast was clear. There was something familiar about those eyes, and I placed them just as he lifted up the beard, giving us a quick flash of his full, handsome face.

"It's me, Sheriff Tucker," he hissed.

Betty recovered quickly from her surprise and rolled her eyes.

"And you thought *that*..." She paused and pointed at Tucker, taking in his entire body with a sweep of her hand. "...was an appropriate way to be dressed when coming to investigate a death?"

Tucker's cheeks reddened, ironically making him look more like Santa than ever.

"I've been volunteering to be Santa at the children's hospital over at Elmsworth," he said, referring to a neighbouring town. "That's why I took awhile to get here and why I'm wearing this costume."

"Well, could you at least take the beard and the hat off? This is a serious matter, Sheriff," Betty said.

She spat the word "Sheriff" like it pained her to refer to

Tucker that way. Perhaps it did. Tucker's heart was in the right place but, unfortunately, his brain didn't always get the memo and it tended to get lost easily.

As Betty spoke, the wail of approaching sirens rent the air. It seemed the ambulance was finally arriving. It always took awhile to get emergency services in Hillbilly Hollow because most of them had to come from Elmsworth. The Hollow was too small to have its own hospital; we only had our little day clinic.

Tucker clicked into professional mode and told Betty, "This whole park needs to be shut down. Maybe it can re-open tomorrow once my deputies and I have had a chance to examine the scene, but for now we need the area cleared."

As if summoned by his words, there came the sound of another set of sirens, undoubtedly Tucker's deputies showing up.

I wasn't in the least bit confident Tucker would have any answers by next month, let alone tomorrow, but I bit my tongue.

Betty beckoned to a volunteer. "Get everyone out. The park is closed for the day and will be re-opening tomorrow," she said.

"But why?" the young volunteer made the mistake of asking.

"Because I said so, that's why," Betty snapped. "Do I need to repeat myself?"

"No," the girl replied.

She hurried off to do Betty's bidding. As much as I didn't appreciate Betty's way of talking to people, I had to admit she had a knack for getting things done. Even as we approached the deer pen, the last few park visitors were being herded out of the Christmas Garden and the gates were being locked.

When the paramedics hurried past, guided by Betty toward the reindeer pen, Tucker finally removed his hat and beard, stuffing them inside his red coat and making his padded stomach look even bigger.

"So what happened?" he asked us all. "Who found the body?"

"I did," Betty replied. "Frank Clarkson was supposed to be looking after the reindeer when they all escaped from their pen. I went to find him to demand to know what had happened, but I discovered him dead on the ground inside the pen."

Tucker walked into the pen but kept back from Frank's body, as the paramedics checked for signs of life. It was obvious even to me that there were none.

Tucker nodded his head toward the scene and told Betty, "Yes, I think I see what happened here. One of the deer must have kicked the victim in the back of the head. I had an uncle who once got kicked in the head by a mule. Knocked half his brains clean out, it did. Yep. The reindeer will have to be destroyed, of course."

I felt my heart sink as Tucker cheerfully related his grisly story. I hadn't expected a lot from him in terms of real detective work, but this was bad, even for him. And there was no way I could keep quiet and let the innocent reindeer be put down.

"Are you serious?" I asked.

"Of course," he replied, looking confused by the question. "It's the most obvious explanation."

There was so much wrong with his theory that I barely knew where to start.

"Tucker, a reindeer didn't do this," I said. "Look at the

body. It's lying on its side. If a reindeer had kicked Frank, don't you think it would have happened while he was approaching the animal, putting the wound on the front or the side of his face? Instead, this blow came from the back."

Tucker considered this, watching as his deputies scattered around us to examine the area and tape off the crime scene.

"Hmm, maybe," he said.

I continued. "Reindeer probably don't have that much force in their kicks, either. Besides, look at the size of the wound compared to a reindeer's hoof. There's no way a reindeer could have done this, Tucker."

"But then why would the reindeer stampede?" Tucker frowned.

I said, "They didn't stampede. They aren't violent animals. They were running around, and granted it caused chaos, but it's only because they were afraid when we all started chasing them."

I pointed to the latch on the gate. "Look, it's not broken. They didn't break out. The gate was left open, probably by whoever did this, hoping to create a distraction and buy themselves time to escape the scene."

Tucker came back over to where I stood just outside the pen. He examined the latch, opening and closing the gate a few times. He shook the gate, testing to see how solid it was, then he nodded his head.

"You might be right, Emma," he said. "Betty, what do you think?"

Betty seemed preoccupied. "I think this place will at least run a lot smoother without Frank Clarkson around to keep upsetting the apple cart," she grumbled.

I frowned. It definitely hadn't taken Betty long to find her acid tongue again.

To her credit, even she looked surprised and then embarrassed at the gruff words that had escaped her mouth. She nodded toward me and admitted grudgingly, "But Emma is probably right. The reindeer didn't do this. They aren't capable of it."

I breathed a sigh of relief. The reindeer would be safe, and whoever had really committed this crime would be brought to justice. Hopefully.

Tucker re-entered the pen now and went closer to Frank's body, moving past the paramedics. Crouching down to peer at the wound, he reached forward and touched the area around it.

I cringed, noticing that he wasn't wearing gloves. He had already contaminated the crime scene when he waded through the pen, and now he had contaminated the area of the wound too.

Tucker stood back up. "After the coroner carries out his post mortem we'll know more. It's obvious old Frank died from a blunt force trauma to the head, but the report should be able to give us a bit more detail about the murder weapon. Meanwhile, did anyone see anything today that might give a clue as to who did this?"

None of the volunteers who had gathered around spoke up.

"Okay then," Tucker said when no one responded. "How about suspicious behaviour of any kind?"

That got me thinking. Of course there was Betty. Her behaviour was strange. She'd had that argument with Frank not long before he was killed, and she wasn't exactly sorry to see him dead. She had been the first one on the scene, which meant she had plenty of time to have opened the gate and shooed the reindeer out. She just had to wait until they were causing the maximum amount of chaos and then start screaming to draw a crowd.

I had suspected Betty of murder once before, though, because of her seemingly cold reaction to Preacher Jacob's murder several months back, and I had ultimately been way off base. That time, the killer had wound up being someone very different. That didn't mean she hadn't done this, of course, but I wanted something more to go on than a hunch if I was going to tell Tucker I thought Betty was suspicious, especially with her standing right beside me.

There was also the woman in the green coat from earlier. It was quite a leap for me to think that someone vandalising a mural was a murderer, but Tucker had only asked if we had seen anything suspicious, and she definitely stood out to me as suspicious. Would she have had time to kill Frank and open the pen, though? Or would she have already been in the middle of spraying her paint when the murder took place? Anyway, no matter how I played it out in my head, I couldn't imagine why she would have killed Frank Clarkson, released the reindeer, and then stopped to vandalise the mural. It just didn't make sense.

There were way too many holes in either of my theories of who the killer might be for me to mention them to Tucker. He was likely to ignore me completely or not want my interference. I was a bit unsure of the sheriff these days anyway, and didn't want to step on his toes.

We hadn't exactly had the most comfortable relationship since our recent trip to New York together. Through a misunderstanding, Tucker had accompanied me on what he mistakenly thought was a romantic trip that ended with me solving the murder of my former landlady. It also ended with me having to set Tucker straight on the fact that our acquaintance was nothing more than a casual friendship.

To his credit, he had treated me ever since as if the whole thing had never happened. Knowing Tucker, he may have actually forgotten it ever *did* happen. Still, I didn't want to push my luck now by telling him how to do his job.

"I haven't seen anything strange," I said to Tucker's question.

"You took a long time to answer that, Emma," Betty pointed out.

"And yet I still answered before you," I couldn't resist saying.

Betty bristled.

"Now now, ladies," Tucker said smoothly. "No need to get upset."

It was an odd thing to say while he stood with the body of a man who had most likely been murdered lying on the ground behind him, but that was Tucker for you.

Now Betty had drawn attention to my pause, I felt like I had to explain it.

"I was just thinking about the lights being vandalised," I said. "But it can't be related, right?"

"Of course not," Betty said, rolling her eyes. "Honestly, Emma. As if children did this. Stop with the theories before you waste Sheriff Tucker's time."

The fact that Betty still hadn't answered Tucker's question was certainly raising my suspicions about her. As though she had read my mind, she turned to Tucker.

"I've seen nothing either, Sheriff," she said. "The ironic thing is that if the victim had been anyone else, I would have been sending you to talk to Frank as a suspect. He was a very angry little man."

She let that thought hang in the air for a moment, before continuing. "Now if you'll excuse me, I have things to do. I have a Santa to cancel. Sheriff, this fair will be re-opening tomorrow as discussed, so I suggest you have your people clear everything away." She waved a hand in the general direction of the crime scene, as if the murder victim was an inconvenient mess to be tidied away.

Then she walked off with her head held high, carrying herself like a woman who was used to being obeyed.

Most of the other staff had gone home while we were talking to Tucker. There was no reason to hang around, really. Colin and Marty remained, working together on fixing the apple cider stand. It didn't feel right for me to just walk away.

As if reading my mind, Tucker said, "It's fine, Emma. You get going. We'll take care of everything here. And don't forget to call me if you think of anything that might help, okay?"

I nodded absently. "Yes. Yes, of course," I said, before heading for the parking lot.

This chance to go home early would give me plenty of time to split tomorrow's firewood in advance, maybe allowing me an extra hour in bed in the morning. And I would have all evening to work on my pitch for Eva for the design work on the Baron's Construction rebrand. I didn't like the tragic reason I had been given the extra time, but that didn't mean I wouldn't make full use of it.

I arrived back at the farm and returned my grandpa's truck keys. I wandered through to the kitchen where I could smell all kinds of delicious aromas wafting. The thick scent of roasting meat mixed with the sweetness of a cake. I inhaled deeply, enjoying the smell.

"What are you making?" I asked as I walked into the kitchen.

"Emma, you're back early," my grandma exclaimed. "I'm

making a steak pie and a chocolate cake for dinner. Both your grandpa's favourites."

"And mine," I said, my stomach growling.

I was surprised. It was barely two hours since I had last eaten, and in the interim I'd seen a dead body. Still, the stomach wants what the stomach wants.

"Why are you home so soon?" Grandma pressed, turning to face me, a spoon coated with chocolate in her hand.

She saw me eying the spoon and handed it over to me. I sat down and licked the gooey goodness, enjoying the sweetness on my tongue. It took me back to my childhood, when murder wasn't even something I knew happened.

"Frank Clarkson was killed. Murdered," I said. "Tucker closed the Christmas Garden down until tomorrow."

"Murdered you say?" Grandma asked, looking shocked. "Well, I never. You know this town was always safe in the old days, but now we've had so much crime in such a short time. It's like we've been cursed or something."

"Maybe I brought you bad luck," I said.

Grandma clucked her tongue. "Now, I'll hear none of that nonsense, young lady. It's just a sign of the times, I guess. Youngsters these days have no respect for their elders. That's the problem."

I refrained from pointing out that the most recent murderers in the town had been far from youngsters. I finished licking the spoon and added it to the washing up bowl with the other utensils Grandma had dirtied. It seemed as though she had managed to use every single spoon, plate and bowl that she owned.

It looked like my wood chopping would have to wait. Instead of going out to the yard, I rolled my sleeves up and began filling the washing up bowl. Grandma watched me for a moment.

"Are you alright, Emma? You know, after what happened?"

I nodded. "Yes. I didn't find him or anything. Betty Blackwell did. The reindeer were loose, and we think whoever killed Frank released them to cause a distraction. I was off helping the others recapture the deer."

Grandma made the clucking sound again. "Typical that Betty Blackwell was the one not helping with that."

A laugh burst out of me at the thought of old Betty running around chasing a reindeer.

Grandma raised her eyebrow and I shook my head.

"She is getting on a bit, Grandma," I pointed out.

"She's younger than me. You think I couldn't catch a reindeer if I wanted to?"

"Honestly Grandma, I think you could catch one much more efficiently than I could," I conceded.

I went back to washing the dishes.

"Where's Snowball?" I asked after a few more minutes. It was strange being in the kitchen without my little white shadow.

"She followed your grandpa out to the fields. Ornery thing that she is, I was glad to get her out of the house. She's obviously made her impression on you, though."

"She has," I agreed.

Who would have thought the big city girl would get attached to a goat? Maybe I really was a country girl at heart.

The rest of the afternoon flew by in a blur of chores. By the time Grandpa came in from the fields and we sat down to the lovely meal Grandma prepared, I was already exhausted, but I knew I had to stay awake and do what needed to be done.

I had to make a living somehow and I needed to complete the quote for Eva. She wasn't going to be in a rush to work with me if I couldn't even meet the deadline for the quote. And the stinkin' firewood. I had to get that split too. The only thing worse I could think of would be having to do it in the morning in the freezing cold.

Grandpa finished his cake and beamed at Grandma. "That was mighty delicious, Dorothy," he said.

Then he yawned and stretched. "Well, I might make an early night of it, I think. It's been a busy day."

He stood up and kissed first Grandma and then me on the cheek. "Good night," he said.

"Night, Grandpa," I replied.

"I'll be up in a bit," Grandma said.

As soon as Grandpa left the room, Grandma turned to me.

"Do you think he's alright?" she asked. "It's not like him to go straight to bed after dinner. Usually says it gives him heartburn."

I said, "He's fine. It's only an hour or so earlier than you would both go to bed anyway, and he's probably stuffed to bursting with coming back for seconds on the pie and the cake."

Grandma laughed. "You're probably right, Emma," she admitted.

Snowball, who had been lying down underneath the table ever since she followed Grandpa back from the fields, stood up and nuzzled her head against my knees.

I laughed and tickled the stop of her head and behind her ears. "You want to be friends again now, huh?" I said to her. "Now that Grandpa's gone to bed, you're coming back to me?"

Grandma stood up. "Emma, would you be a dear and clean up in here? I'm sure you're right about your grandpa, but I'd like to go up and just make sure everything's okay with him. Plus, I'm extra tired myself tonight."

"Sure," I said, even though I could see my own bedtime getting later and later.

Two and a half hours later, the kitchen was spotless and my quote and the explanation of exactly what I would do for Eva was done and sent.

"Let's go collect some wood," I said to Snowball.

She followed me across the kitchen and out the back door. She ran gaily across the yard, her little tail flicking back and forth, a patch of white in the black of night. It was almost like she had understood me, because she headed straight for the woodpile.

But she had only gone partway when she suddenly stopped her joyful trotting and bleating, coming to a standstill. After a second, she lay down quietly in the grass and couldn't be coaxed to go further. I knew then.

I had learned to expect the appearance of ghosts after every violent death in town. Ever since the murder of Preacher Jacob, ghosts of the unjustly killed seemed drawn to me like magnets. And, somehow, Snowball could usually sense the presence of ghosts. If she wouldn't go a step closer to the woodshed, that likely meant I could expect to find a ghostly presence there.

I left her behind and rounded the outhouse. Sure enough, a figure stood in the darkness. I felt a chill run down my spine. What if I was wrong and this wasn't an apparition but an axe murderer?

Get a grip, Emma, I told myself, stepping closer. How

many murderers could be running around town at once? The odds said more than one was unlikely.

A cloud shifted from across the moon, moved by the gentle night breeze, and I saw that my visitor was indeed Frank.

He seemed paler and gaunter now than he had been when he was alive, but then dying and coming back as an apparition was bound to change a person.

"You have to help me," he demanded irritably at my approach. "I can't move on until I know who did this to me."

There was no greeting and no explanation of why he had chosen me to appear to, I noticed. Frank was as gruff in death as he had been in life.

I adopted a similar attitude, folding my arms. I wasn't going to be pushed around by a dead man. But I also had a duty to the dead and no need of explanation. My special gift had given me the responsibility of finding justice for the unjustly killed and I had accepted it some time ago.

"Do you have any idea who it was that murdered you?" I asked him, barely even fazed by the craziness of standing in the backyard chatting with a ghost. This had become normal for me. "Did you see anything?"

"Not a thing," he replied. "I was just standing there, minding my own business like, when I felt a massive wallop to the back of my head. Everything went black. Next thing I know, I'm dead."

He seemed to be getting agitated, and I decided an agitated ghost wasn't a good ghost. Who knew what might happen if he got really angry?

"Don't worry, Frank. I'll find out who did this and get you justice," I replied. I knew that was what he had come to ask of me. It was what the ghosts always asked.

"Don't take too long," he ordered, as he began to fade away.

He was gone within two or three seconds. Snowball jumped back up and began her happy bleating again. It proved he was gone, and I turned to Snowball and voiced my concern.

"Did I just make a promise I can't keep?"

I hoped not. And if I was honest with myself, I was pleased to have made the promise. It gave me an excuse to investigate what had really happened to Frank, something I had been itching to do all along.

7

T he next morning, I felt strangely excited when I made my way down the stairs and out to the woodpile. Not about the wood chopping. No, it would never be about that. I still had a hate-hate relation-ship with the woodpile, and I didn't see that changing until summer came around again and I no longer had to go near it. My excitement was about helping Frank Clarkson.

When I had first started seeing ghosts, they used to frighten me. Partly because I thought I was going crazy. But it seemed like somewhere along the way I had mostly gotten over being scared. I hadn't felt freaked out after Frank's visit, and I wasn't jumping at shadows, waiting for something else to happen. I had no reason to fear this ghost.

Unless you break your promise, a little voice whispered in the back of my mind.

Well then, I'd better make sure I don't, I whispered back, as I lugged as big a pile of wood as I could carry into the kitchen and headed back for another load.

The cold air seeped into my bones and I shivered, despite the thick coat I wore and the heavy lifting I was doing. Winter was definitely here, and the thin flurries of snow that had begun during the night promised it was only going to get colder. And if Grandpa was right about the snow, then this was only the start of it.

I took a moment to look out at the farm. It was still quiet and peaceful at this time of the morning, with not even the lowing of a cow or the crowing of a rooster to break up the silence. The snow shone in the faint light as it gently floated to the ground. I felt like I was standing in a snow globe.

I smiled to myself as I made what I hoped would be the last trip back to the house with my arms full of wood. If I'd seen flurries like this back in New York, my heart would have sunk. It would have meant delayed transport, more crowds, and the certainty of being late, no matter how early I set off. Now it meant hot cocoa in front of the roaring fire with a good book, not a care in the world, and Christmas magic twinkling on the ground and in the trees.

"I'm going soft, Snowball," I whispered when I saw the little goat appear.

She bleated in response and rubbed her head on my legs, forcing me to stop walking.

"I can't pet you with all of this firewood in my arms," I informed her.

As if she understood, she moved to one side and stood looking at me expectantly, her little white tail whipping up a storm. I shook my head in amusement and hurried back to the house before she changed her mind and refused to move until I'd scratched behind her ears. The only thing worse than lighting up the stove would be attempting to light up the stove with wet firewood.

By the time I'd put the wood into the burner, my hands were just about defrosted, although my skin was red and chapped. I was about to make a move toward

Grandma's kitchen drawer and the hidden stash of newspaper there, but before I could, I heard footsteps from above. They were heavy steps that meant Grandpa was up.

Now I'd have to do the fire the hard way, and under his watchful eye, too. If only I'd been five minutes earlier, the fire would be going now and the evidence of the paper gone, already turned to ashes.

"Morning," Grandpa grunted as he came into the kitchen. "It's freezin' in here. What have you been doing?"

"I got caught up watching the snow fall," I admitted.

Grandpa's face softened. "You always did like the snow," he commented.

He watched me for a moment as I tried and failed to light the fire. Then he shook his head and moved to a cupboard, where he pulled out a blue toolbox. He opened it up and produced a few sheets of newspaper.

I raised my eyebrows as he began balling up the paper.

He saw me looking and grinned sheepishly. "This makes it so much quicker and easier to get the fire started. Just don't be tellin' your grandma I cheat at this, you hear me? She's a natural at this stuff, and she thinks I am too. It won't hurt to have it stay that way."

I nodded, trying to suppress a grin. If only they both knew the other one employed the same trick.

"Mum's the word," I promised as Grandpa put the paper in the burner and lit it.

"There," he said, satisfied that the fire was going to take. "You can use this, but if you use the last sheet, replace it. And if your grandma catches you, I'll deny all knowledge of it. Are we clear?"

I nodded again and Grandpa smiled, before changing the subject.

"How's that job of yours going? The design one?" he asked.

"Really well, thanks." I beamed. "Eva loved my design ideas and she's accepted my quote. I'll be working on that until probably Christmas so that'll keep me out of mischief."

"I think it'll take more than that. Your grandma said you witnessed a murder yesterday at the Christmas Garden. Old Frank Clarkson?"

"I didn't witness any such thing, Grandpa. You know how Grandma exaggerates. By the time she tells her friends in the quilting club, she'll probably have me down as the murderer. Frank really was killed, though. It makes you think, doesn't it? I mean, I know he could be an old grouch at times, but for someone to do that to him..."

I trailed off, once more thinking about Betty Blackwell and the woman in the green coat.

"Sad business," Grandpa commented. "You stay safe working down there at the park, Emma. No nosing around the way you do. Just leave the Sheriff to deal with this."

"Tucker? He tried to say the reindeer did it, Grandpa."

"Well then, that's a problem, but it's not *your* problem. Frank is gone whether Tucker finds his killer or not."

I knew I'd never talk Grandpa around to my way of thinking, but I tried a different approach just the same.

"People will be scared with a killer on the loose," I commented.

"That they will be," he agreed. "But catching that killer is a job for professionals."

"True," I commented.

I wasn't lying, I told myself. Grandpa was right. When the time came, there were other people whose job it was to arrest Frank's murderer. Only I didn't exactly promise not to do my part.

8

I hurried across the parking lot and rushed into Hollow Heights. Betty spotted me as I passed through the Christmas Garden entrance gate.

"Nice of you to join us, Emma," she said coolly.

"Thank you. You know me, always glad to help out," I said.

I kept my voice cheery and innocent, although I was getting a little bit tired of her incessant criticism. I was only five minutes later than I had said I'd be. With the snow coming thicker and faster, she must have understood that the roads were moving slowly. But maybe my sweet response would at least make her feel guilty.

Despite what Tucker had said about reopening in a day, I hadn't really even expected to be here again so soon after Frank's murder. I'd spent the morning helping Grandma and Grandpa around the farm, and after lunch, I'd gone up to my room to work on Eva's designs.

Betty had called just as I'd gotten settled in with my laptop fired up. She'd informed me that Tucker had ruled the park safe and asked if I was free to come in. I'd debated saying no, but I thought of all the work that I'd put into the preparations and found myself agreeing. It was only for two weeks, I had told myself. Less than two weeks, really.

"Well, you're here now," Betty said in a more agreeable voice. Evidently, my effort at guilting her had worked.

I knew it was the closest I would get to an apology and I smiled, willing to meet her halfway.

"So, Tucker has cleared us to reopen the park. Does that mean he knows who killed Frank?" I asked.

"I wouldn't know," Betty said. "It's really none of my business."

Like that would stop her from asking or Tucker from telling her, I thought to myself.

Betty continued. "However, I would hazard a guess that no one has been arrested yet, since Sheriff Tucker has posted a deputy to patrol the area and keep everyone feeling safe."

I raised an eyebrow.

"Oh, don't worry. I'm sure there won't be any more violence," Betty said.

Because you killed Frank and you're not planning to kill again?

I mentally chastised myself for the suspicious thought. Betty was only trying to put my mind at rest, after all.

"I'm sure it'll be fine," I agreed. "I'm just surprised that Tucker thought to post somebody, that's all."

Betty shrugged. "I imagine he only suggested it as a means of making visitors feel at ease. Nobody wants to attend a park event where they feel unsafe."

I had to admit that much was true. The Christmas Garden could well flop after what had happened. People might be wary about coming here so soon after a murder had taken place, especially those with children. The sight of a deputy's uniform should prove reassuring. On a more practical note, I also hoped having a deputy around the park would stop any more acts of vandalism.

"You're on ice rink duty again," Betty said, back in efficient leader mode. "Hurry along to your station now."

She practically shooed me away, and I had to hide a smile of amusement as it made me think of Grandma chasing the chickens around the coop.

I put Betty from my mind for awhile and got to work.

9

The next couple of hours were pretty uneventful. The park got a lot busier than I was expecting, and I decided to give Tucker a little credit. Although the deputy he'd sent seemed more interested in hot cocoa and candied apples than in keeping an eye out for trouble, his presence seemed to be having the desired effect. Frank's murder was still a hot topic of conversation, but people seemed more curious than afraid.

Remembering my promise to the ghost of Frank, I did some subtle asking around among the volunteers to see if anybody knew much about Frank and any possible enemies he might have. Unfortunately, I was unsuccessful in finding out anything useful. The bits of information I heard contained nothing of interest, and I worried that if I asked too many questions, people would grow suspicious that I was up to something.

My grandma had mentioned that she and "the girls," as she called them, would be by after their quilting session today. I was biding my time, waiting for them to arrive. They were all big gossips, so a lot of what they said had to be taken with a pinch of salt, but if there were any skeletons in Betty Blackwell's closet, they would be the ones to know about it.

And if the woman in the green coat was known to the townsfolk, I might be able to learn something about her too. I'd kept my eyes peeled all day watching for the vandal who'd destroyed the mural, but I hadn't seen any sign of her. Of course, I'd never gotten a look at her face, so she could have walked right up to me and stood chatting and, if she was wearing anything but that familiar green coat, I wouldn't have known who I was talking to.

I had spotted one green coat earlier on and dashed off into the crowd, unsure of what I would say when I caught up with its wearer, but needing to act all the same. Before I could confront her, she had turned around and I recognised her as the mayor's wife. It was too farfetched even for me to believe the mayor's wife was involved in vandalism and possibly murder, so I had returned quietly to my spot at the ice rink.

Later, I glimpsed Grandma and her friends through the crowd. They were talking nonstop, giggling like school girls, and it made me smile to see Grandma so laid back and happy. She was the picture of young at heart. When she was like this, it was easy to see what Grandpa meant about her funny spells being no big deal. It would surely be wrong to make her think she was anything but the fit young thing she felt like.

Grandma spotted me and waved. She headed over, the others following.

"Hi, ladies. How's it going, Grandma?" I said.

"Two tickets please." Grandma beamed.

"What? Oh, you mean for the raffle? I'm not selling those

tickets, Grandma. You want Simon. I'm selling tickets for the ice rink."

"I know," Grandma said, nodding. "Rose and I are going for a skate. Right, Rose?"

Rose, a woman older than my grandma by a few years, had weathered the storm of life almost as well as Grandma, but the idea of them ice skating shocked me.

"Sure as grass is green," Rose answered my grandma solemnly.

"But what if you fall?" I blurted out.

"Fall schmall," Grandma said. "Now are you going to sell me those tickets or do I have to go and report you to Betty Blackwell?"

She smiled triumphantly as I raised my hands in mock surrender.

"You win," I said with a smile. "Two tickets it is."

I watched, still not quite believing what I was seeing, as Grandma and Rose sat down and removed their shoes and put skates on. I half closed my eyes as they stepped onto the ice. I needn't have worried. After a little wobble, Grandma was off. She skated around the rink as skilfully as any of the kids around her. I was almost waiting for her to attempt a double axel spin.

I glanced over at Rose. She seemed a little unsure, standing at the edge, watching Grandma.

"Come on, Rosie! Show these kids how it's done!" Grandma laughed as she sailed past her friend.

Rose shrugged and pushed off from the edge. I felt my jaw drop as she skated. She turned and began to skate backwards, so fast she was hard to keep track of.

"Well, I'll be..." Diana said from behind me, her voice full of slightly amused awe. "I thought they were pulling our legs when they said they were going to go skating and show everyone it wasn't just a kid's game."

"Me too," Jane said. "Good to know there's still life in some of us oldies yet."

Margene was less interested in watching the skaters than in making conversation. "So Emma, terrible business you finding old Frank Clarkson's body. Your grandma was telling us all about it," she said to me.

This was the opening I had been waiting for. "Actually, it was Betty Blackwell who found the body. I heard her scream and went to see what was wrong. It's funny that Betty should have been the one to discover the crime. She seemed to have a bit of a grudge against Frank anyway, didn't she?"

Margene threw her head back and laughed. "Find me someone Betty Blackwell doesn't have a grudge against and I'll show you someone she hasn't met yet."

It was a fair point. Betty wasn't exactly sociable.

As if to prove Margene's point, Betty herself appeared at the edge of the nearby woods, shouting at a young woman who was busy stringing up a few more lights. The girl stood in apparent shock, listening to Betty's rant and occasionally nodding her head. Betty stormed away, frowning, leaving the girl looking both amused and slightly lost for words.

Diane joined in the gossip then. "It's true that Betty particularly disliked Frank, though. You don't think ...?" Her voice left the words unsaid but her eyes asked the question anyway. Clearly, the possibility of Betty Blackwell as a murderer was too juicy not to entertain.

"What? No, goodness no. Of course not," I said, feigning surprise. "I just thought it was ironic that Frank's last act was to almost give Betty a heart attack when she found his body, that's all."

It wouldn't do to have these ladies telling the whole

town that Betty was Frank's killer. I wasn't even sure I thought that myself. I needed more evidence before I could form a definite opinion about it.

"If you ask me, this whole business stinks of Harold Abbott," Ethel put in.

"Harold Abbott, who used to work at the Broadway Street Bakery?" I asked in surprise.

I was vaguely familiar with the older man because Grandma used to take me into his delicious bakery when I was a teenager, before the place closed down. My grandparents had been on chatty terms with Mr. Abbott but I mostly just knew him by sight.

Ethel nodded. She moved closer, her blue eyes twinkling at having a captive audience to share her theory with.

I spotted Diane rolling her eyes behind Ethel. It was clear Ethel's circle of friends were sick of hearing whatever story she was going to tell me.

"Harold and Frank, they feuded for years," Ethel said. "They lived next door to each other, you know. Harold Abbott is a proud man, likes to keep up appearances and all that. His lawn and garden are always immaculate, and his home is beautiful. He busied himself with its upkeep after his wife died a few years back. Poor Helen loved puttering around in that garden, rest her soul. Anyway, Frank didn't share Harold's sentiment about keeping up property. His own yard was awful overgrown, with all sorts of trash lying around. Harold took that as a personal insult, and he regularly accused Frank of sullying his wife's memory. Wouldn't surprise me if he'd confronted Frank about whatever bee was in his bonnet at the time, and the fight went too far."

The theory was interesting. I had to give Ethel high marks for imagination. It was quite a stretch to think anyone would kill over a messy yard, of course, but if

Harold Abbott thought the mess was somehow an insult to his dead wife, that might make it a little more believable. At any rate, it wasn't like my own ideas about Betty Blackwell and the green-coated woman were much better.

The biggest problem with the Abbott theory was that I hadn't actually seen Harold Abbott anywhere in the park on the day of the murder. But that didn't mean he wasn't there. He could have sneaked in, did what he had to do to Frank and then slipped away in the chaos.

Anyway, my other suspects were awfully weak. The timing was tight, to say the least, with the woman in the green coat. And surely Betty Blackwell would have let someone else find Frank's body, if she'd killed him? Why call attention to herself by being the one to find him?

"Emma?" Margene cut in. "Are you listening to me?"

"What? Oh, sorry. Go on," I said, blushing.

"I said you should pay Ethel no mind. She's never forgiven Harold for the year he forgot to add chocolate chips to her birthday cake at the old bakery, and she'd say anything to tarnish his reputation."

"Nonsense," Ethel huffed. "It's what Joan Fielder thinks happened. And she was Harold's housekeeper at one time. If she thinks he's capable of murder, then I reckon he is."

I turned my attention back to Grandma and Rose, who were still happily skating. A little girl who was a bit wobbly on her skates was holding Grandma's hand and Grandma was gently encouraging the child, showing her how to keep her balance.

Ethel had given me a lot to think about. I was aware that it was mostly whisperings that had gotten out of hand, the same way the gossip mill had transformed me from someone who was in the park during the murder to the discoverer of the body. But I was in no position to discount a suspect. I had too few of them as it was.

Not that I was quite ready to write off Betty Blackwell or the woman in the green coat just yet. I debated asking Grandma's friends about the green-coated vandal. But to do so, I'd have to admit that I'd seen her damaging the mural and not said anything to Tucker about it when he was asking earlier about suspicious behaviour at the park. No, I was definitely on my own with identifying that mysterious woman.

Grandma and Rose finally left the ice, laughing and clinging to each other like two girls much younger. I was reminded of Suzy and me when we were teens. I shook my head, but I couldn't help but smile, as the pair changed back into their shoes and Grandma came over to me.

"Aren't you about due to leave, Emma?" she asked me.

A plan was brewing in the back of my mind to drive over to Frank Clarkson's place and take a look around, just to see if his property was really bad enough to encourage the sort of neighbour-against-neighbour feud Ethel had mentioned. But I wasn't about to admit that to Grandma.

"Yes," I replied. "I was going to pop into town and see if Suzy is in her store. But if you want a lift home, I could drop you off first."

Grandma shook her head. "No. It's fine, Emma. You just look so cold, that's all," she said.

"Ah, I'm used to it now." I smiled.

The ladies said their goodbyes and wandered off back into the crowd. I dreaded to think what they would get up to next. I was still smiling to myself about Grandma on the ice when I finally headed to the marquee and collected my purse.

Betty was in there with her clipboard, looking important, as always. I noticed she never moved far from the heater that had been set up in the tent. In fairness, I didn't really blame her for that. It was so cold out that my breath was making white plumes in the air.

"Are you here tomorrow, Emma?" Betty asked me as I got myself ready to leave.

I nodded. "Yes, I'll be here every day unless something comes up with my grandparents."

I hurried away, pretending not to hear the harrumphing noise she made to my comment. I crossed the park and got into the truck, before pulling the mirror down. Grandma hadn't been kidding when she'd said I looked cold. My skin was red and mottled and my lips were chapped. I applied a smear of balm that did nothing to improve the ragged look of my lips. The red blotches on my face were already growing as the truck's heater did its job of defrosting me and I moved the mirror back into position to see the road rather than my face.

Before starting off, I pulled my cell phone out and tapped out a text to Suzy.

ME: If my grandma happens 2 come by, tell her I popped in 2 see U.

SUZY: Y? Hot date with Billy?

ME: Ha. Very funny.

I wished she would drop that subject, but I knew the more I insisted she let it go, the more weight it would give to her theory that Billy and I were soul mates.

I stopped thinking about Suzy and Billy, and drove away in the direction of Frank Clarkson's house.

The snow was still falling. The gentle flurries had been replaced with large, fat flakes that fell constantly. The roads were quiet, but the going was still fairly slow because of the slushy streets. The main road through town had been gritted, but it was the only one, and once I was off Main Street I had to slow down almost to a crawl.

If I hadn't already sort of remembered which house belonged to Frank Clarkson, and if the name on the mailbox hadn't been confirmation enough, I could have guessed at the right place from Ethel's description. Two houses at the end of the street stood apart from all the others, joined by one low wall in the back. The lawns of both properties melded, lacking any fence to separate them. It was easy to see which half of the wide expanse belonged to which owner.

Harold Abbott's side, surrounding his beautiful old Victorian house, was carefully manicured. Although his lawn was brown at this time of year, there was no missing the careful arrangement of his flower beds and the elegant shape of the shrubs poking up from beneath their dusting of snow. A large water feature stood in the centre of the lawn, a three tier affair adorned with stone frogs. The water had frozen into a delicate waterfall now, ice cycles cascading down from the tiers.

On Frank's side, drooping brown weeds were abundant, leaning beneath the weight of the snow. Old railroad ties lay scattered in the side yard, maybe part of some project that had never been finished. A dead tree lay across the ground near the sagging steps of the front porch. The closest Frank's lawn came to having a water feature was the abandoned bath tub and an old toilet lying in the corner.

I could see why Mr. Abbott would be upset by the state of Frank's lawn. It must be frustrating to live next to something that looked like a junk yard. But was that really enough of a concern to prompt a murder? Even if the part was true about Harold taking solace in his garden after his wife's death, I had a hard time imagining him murdering his neighbour just because Frank's yard was unsightly.

I slowed the truck down so much I was practically at a stop. I didn't want to draw attention to myself, but a festive looking sign in Harold Abbott's garden had caught my eye. Suddenly, I had a plausible excuse for being there, should he spot me and come out.

The sign was advertising the fact that this home was part of the town's annual Christmas Tour of Historic Homes. Folk in Hillbilly Hollow were short on entertainment sometimes. The Christmas tour gave everyone an excuse to parade through one another's older houses and do a bit of polite snooping, for a price. I had to admit I was tempted to book a place on the tour.

It was true that I had glimpsed Harold Abbott around town a few times since my return from New York. But I certainly didn't know him well enough to knock on his door to talk to him about Frank Clarkson just out of the blue. Being on the tour would give me the perfect excuse to run into him and maybe just casually mention what a shame it was about Frank. Then I could gauge his reaction.

I had made my decision. I stopped the truck altogether and pulled my cell phone out. I typed in the number from the sign and reached a recorded message informing me the booking office was now closed and to try again the next day. I sighed but resolved not to give up easily. I would be back here later.

10

My back felt like it was about ready to break as I straightened up and leaned on my snow shovel, hot pain running along my spine and down my legs. But I was glad I was the one to do this, rather than my grandparents having to.

The snow had continued to fall all night and a thick layer now coated the farmyard. The fields looked beautifully uniform, dazzling white spreading out as far as the eye could see. But the lovely white blanket had brought a curse with it--an icy driveway that I'd had to clear a trail through, leading out to the truck. After my daily fight with the wood burning stove, of course.

I stood back and admired my handiwork. I had done a thorough job of snow shovelling and sprinkling around a little grit, even if I said so myself. But I was sure glad it was done. I made a mental note to keep spreading new layers of grit over the next few days and not let the ice build back up to the point where it all needed clearing again. Once was more than enough.

I checked my watch. I had half an hour before I needed

to head to Hollow Heights. I quickened my pace as I imagined sitting at the kitchen table in the warmth with a lovely big mug of coffee.

It wasn't to be. My cell phone buzzed in my pocket. Suzy. I felt an icy spike of fear. Suzy never called me. She was a texter through and through. For her to call, something bad must have happened. I answered the call.

"Suzy? What is it?"

"Emma, I need your help," Suzy said.

She sounded breathless, and my heart beat faster, anticipating an emergency.

I said, "Of course. What's wrong? What's happened?"

"I'm all out of grit and the town council refuses to send city workers to spread grit outside of private businesses. There's snow everywhere, building back up as fast as I can clear it. I don't suppose your grandparents have a bag of grit to spare, do they? I was hoping you could drop it in on your way to the Christmas Garden."

Relief flooded through me. It was just Suzy being a drama queen.

"That's your big emergency?" I demanded.

"Well yes, what did you think it was? Honestly, Emma, you're so dramatic."

I ignored the irony of her statement and rolled my eyes. "I'll be over soon. I have to get to the park, though, so I won't be able to stay long. Just get some coffee on. I have time for a quick cup of that."

"Deal," Suzy said with a laugh as she hung up.

I went into the house and explained the situation to Grandma. She looked concerned.

"What is it?" I asked.

"The council refusing to help. Never would have happened in my day," she said. "It's an outrage."

I smiled, thinking it was funny the things that consti-
tuted an outrage in a town this small.

"Be careful on the roads, Emma," Grandma warned me
as I headed back out to the porch for a bag of grit.

"I will," I promised her, before the door closed
behind me.

My arms full of the heavy bag, I hurried out to the truck.

I had to slow down, once I pulled out of the driveway,
because the roads were slick. Carefully, I headed for Suzy's
shop.

Suzy was out front when I arrived, supervising as her
teenaged shop assistant shovelled the snow that was coming
down faster than she could scoop it up. That was a little odd,
I thought. It wasn't like Suzy to stand back and let somebody
else do the work. It went against her bossy nature not to
pitch in and take control.

I got out of the truck and began pouring the grit on the
areas already cleared. It didn't take long before the grit
began to do its job. Suzy stood in the doorway grinning at
me, as I came indoors into the warmth of the shop.

"Emma, you're a life saver. Now let's get you that hot
drink you were asking for. I made cocoa instead of coffee. I'd
say you've earned it."

We went inside and Suzy handed me a steaming mug of
cocoa. I took it gratefully and sipped it, the warming aroma
and sweet taste instantly making me feel cozy.

"So? You and Billy, huh?" Suzy grinned, as she slid onto
a stool behind the counter, near the cash register.

"What do you mean?" I asked, setting down my mug
long enough to hop up onto my customary seat atop the
counter.

"Last night. Lying to your grandma," she prompted me.

Oh. I had forgotten about my text to Suzy.

"I wasn't with Billy," I told her.

"Mmmhmm," she said.

"No really, I wasn't," I insisted.

I told her what had happened to Frank Clarkson and where I had been yesterday evening when I'd asked her to cover for me. I just hadn't wanted Grandma stopping by Suzy's shop and wondering why I wasn't where I'd said I would be.

Suzy listened with interest and shook her head. "I hope Tucker knows how lucky he is to have you running around doing his job for him. He'd have been quite happy to blame the reindeer and call it case closed. It's a good thing you've got an intuition about these things."

I opened my mouth and closed it again. I had never really explained to Suzy that I got my information from ghosts, and now didn't seem like the time to share that news.

"I guess playing detective keeps me feeling useful," I said instead.

Suzy abruptly turned the conversation back to Billy. "So no chance of you and Billy having yourselves a little Christmas romance then?"

"No," I said simply, and changed the subject myself. "Speaking of romance, how are you and Brian looking forward to your first Christmas as a married couple?"

Her face lit up and she beamed at me. "Oh Emma, everything is wonderful. Brian really is the best guy a girl could ask for. You know, last night I said I was in the mood for a chocolate bar and he went out in all that snow to get me one."

"He knew he wouldn't get any peace until he did," I said, laughing.

"Well, yeah," Suzy agreed. "But I love that he went without me having to bug him."

I glanced at my watch as I drained the last of my cocoa.

"Well, I have to dash. Betty Blackwell won't let me hear the end of it if I'm late," I said, giving Suzy a quick hug, before heading for the door.

As I got back into the truck and drove away, it hit me that I missed Suzy. I had thought after her wedding we would somehow still continue seeing each other as much as we ever had. But a lot had changed these past few months. It was no use pretending it hadn't. Brian was Suzy's first priority nowadays, and every time I'd text her to do something, she was already busy.

I reminded myself that it was natural for her to want to spend time with her husband. I had no right to mind that she wasn't willing to drop everything the moment I suggested it. I would have to adjust to the change, and get used to seeing a little less of her.

Knowing all of that didn't stop me from feeling suddenly lonely. I had my grandparents, but I needed more than my family. I needed friendship.

In a moment of weakness, before I really knew what I was doing, I pulled the truck to the side of the road and got my cell phone out.

I opened my text messages and found my thread with Billy. I tapped out a text that sounded fake and desperate even to me. I quickly deleted it and wrote a more suitable one.

ME: Hey. What's up? Wanna hang out tonight after the Christmas Garden closes?

I LOOKED AT THE MESSAGE, debating whether or not to send

it. I suddenly realized that if he wrote back saying he was busy I would probably cry. Suzy had moved on without me, but seemingly Billy hadn't. If that changed any time soon, how bad would it hurt?

I shook my head and told myself to stop being so dramatic. People were allowed to have plans that didn't involve me, and if Billy was busy tonight, then it didn't mean anything except it was too short notice to ask him to do something. I pressed send before I could change my mind.

I told myself I ought to get the truck back on the road instead of sitting there clutching my cell phone, willing it to buzz. But I didn't move.

I didn't have long to wait before Billy's reply buzzed in.

What if it was a no? What if he had gotten sick of being brushed off? With a racing heart, I opened the message and relief flooded me.

BILLY: I'd love to. Drop by whenever U R done."

I sent him a smiley emoji and got back on the road. Apparently, I had worried for nothing.

11

I was glad when I was able to get out of the marquee at the fair. Under normal circumstances, taking a break in the warmth would have been welcome, but Betty Blackwell had cornered me in there and taken any fun out of my lunch break.

She had discovered another act of vandalism.

The lights in the trees around the edges of the park had been broken again and Betty had needed to organize a cleanup of all the busted glass and find volunteers to clamber into the trees and hang up fresh strands.

She had ranted about it for a full twenty minutes until she had eventually gotten herself so infuriated that she'd stormed away to call Tucker. I had bitten my tongue to stop myself from pointing out to her that Tucker had a murder to solve and it would surely take precedence over a few broken lights. Or, knowing Tucker, maybe it wouldn't. I could definitely see the mystery of the vandalized lights occupying far too much of Tucker's time.

Maybe that was why Betty was so eager to report it, a niggling voice in the back of my head whispered, as I ducked out of the tent. Maybe Betty broke the lights herself so she could keep Tucker distracted from the murder investigation. Maybe she was somehow responsible for all the vandalism happening around the park lately. But that wouldn't mesh with what my own eyes had told me, when I'd caught the green-coated woman painting that graffiti over the mural.

As I walked through the biting cold back towards the candy cane stand I was manning today, I saw something through the milling crowd that made me look twice.

There was nothing unusual about the middle-aged man in a brown sweater and plaid scarf, hovering around a big evergreen tree strewn with lights. With his thinning dark hair and the camera in his hand, he looked just like the many other park visitors who came to the Christmas Garden to photograph the decorative displays. But there was one remarkable thing about this particular park visitor.

He was Harold Abbott. The same Harold Abbott who had lived next door to the dead Frank Clarkson.

Considering the gossip I had heard about the feud between Mr. Abbott and the murder victim, and considering how recently I had sat in front of Harold Abbott's house, scheming about how to get inside it to question him or look around for clues, this coincidence was almost too good to be true.

My heart sped up a little bit at the sight of him. Was it a case of the murderer returning to the scene of the crime? Or was it more a case of a lonely man wanting to enjoy some community spirit and Christmas cheer?

I couldn't pass up the opportunity to talk to him and maybe find out. I changed direction and veered towards him in what I hoped was a casual way. I hung back while he finished snapping pictures of the tree and slipped his camera into his sweater pocket. Then I followed and watched as he approached a refreshment stand. He bought himself a cup of hot chocolate. I waited until he turned around, warming his hands on the cup.

I smiled at him and stepped closer.

"Hi, Mr. Abbott," I said.

"Hello," he replied.

I guessed from his formal tone that he had no memory of who I was, not surprising since I had only been back in town a few months, and we'd never known each other well anyway. I knew he would keep his guard all the way up if he thought I was a total stranger. It was the small town mentality. I hoped name dropping my grandparents would be enough to convince him I was a born and raised Hillbilly Hollow girl, not an outsider. It was usually enough.

"You probably don't remember me, but I used to stop by your bakery all the time with my grandma when I was young," I said. "I'm Emma, Ed and Dorothy Hooper's granddaughter."

"Oh. Emma. Of course." He smiled politely. "I heard you were back in town. How are you finding our sleepy way of life?"

"Anything but sleepy," I replied honestly. "Between the farm and the Christmas Garden, I barely have time to sleep."

"Ah, well, it's always best to be active. It stops you having to think too much," he said, with a note of sadness.

I didn't really know what to say to that and the comment hung heavily in the air between us. He cleared his throat, looking uncomfortable, and gave me another half smile.

"Well, I should let you get on," he said.

I couldn't allow him to just walk away. I hadn't even broached the subject of Frank yet.

"I wanted to ask you something, actually," I blurted out.

"Oh?" he asked with a raised eyebrow.

"I saw that your home was included in the Historic Homes Christmas Tour. I wondered how it felt, you know, to have people in your personal space, discovering all of your secrets."

I laughed as I said it, hoping to make it sound less ominous, but I really wanted to gauge his reaction.

He merely smiled gently.

"Oh, I think secrets are few and far between in a town like ours. Everyone knows each other, and with that, everyone knows everyone else's business. I honestly enjoy welcoming interested people into my home. I work hard on keeping the house and garden to a high standard. If other people enjoy seeing that, who am I to deny them the pleasure?"

My soft approach clearly wasn't working. If I wanted him to talk about Frank it was clear to me that I would have to be the one to bring him up.

"It's such a shame about your neighbour, Frank Clarkson. I hope the scandal doesn't put people off taking part in the tour," I said, choosing my words carefully.

Harold Abbott tilted his head to one side. "Well, you know what people around here are like. If anything, the tragedy may draw more crowds wanting to get a glimpse of the house of a murder victim next door."

I nodded in agreement. I couldn't risk making him suspicious by asking how he felt personally about the death of Frank. Not when I still had a thousand and one other questions for him. I decided to move the conversation back to safer ground.

"I was actually thinking about taking the tour myself," I said.

Mr. Abbott beamed with pride, so I decided to amp it up one more step and really play to his ego.

I said, "Of course I'd have to start with your home ahead of all the other houses on the tour. It's by far the most beautiful and I think it has real historic relevance to the town."

I had no idea if that was even remotely true or not, but Harold Abbott was obviously lapping it up, as any proud home owner might. He dug around in his pocket with a gloved hand and clumsily pushed a piece of paper towards me.

"Here. I have a few tickets to hand out. This one is for tomorrow night's tour of my home. If you can, drop by and make use of it."

"Oh, thank you, I will," I replied, a little touched by the awkward display of generosity.

I pushed the ticket into my pocket, feeling slightly guilty at getting the freebie in this way. If its giver had any idea why I really wanted into his house, he might not be so kind.

"I'd best get on now," Harold Abbott said. "Enjoy the tour."

He merged back into the crowd before I could say anything else.

I was glad to know that now I had a conversation starter if I bumped into him again later. I could just talk about how lovely his home was and he'd be putty in my hands.

And yet, I shouldn't let myself get carried away with exploring the depth of Mr. Abbott's feud with the murder victim. My suspicions could be way off. After all, if you'd killed a man, and someone started asking questions about your relationship with the dead guy, even general ones, would you be so quick to invite them to tour your house? I was sure I wouldn't be.

I was pulled abruptly from my thoughts when I

glimpsed a flash of red through the crowd. It took me a second to realize it was Tucker, once again dressed in his Santa suit. His appearance was causing quite a stir with the children in the park.

Tucker spotted me in the same moment I saw him and he waved.

I waved back and waited for him to reach me, smiling at the excited whispers that rippled through the children as he passed them by.

"Hi Emma," he said when he reached me. "I just wanted to make sure you were okay. You know, after the whole Frank Clarkson business."

"I'm fine, thanks. I mean, it was a shock, but yeah, I'm alright now. I hope the case is moving toward a speedy resolution?"

Tucker looked left and right, as though to check that no one was listening in.

I felt my heart speed up a little. He was obviously going to tell me something important. Maybe the police actually knew who the killer was.

"The coroner's report just came back. Frank was killed by blunt force trauma to the head," Tucker whispered.

I let out the breath I had been holding. So much for new developments. The whole town already knew how Frank had died. The question everyone wanted an answer to was *who* had caused the trauma.

But I nodded, hoping to encourage Tucker to continue. "How about suspects? Do you have any leads on the murderer?"

At that point, Tucker must have remembered that I was a civilian and not one of his deputies, because he reverted to the official sounding line, "Now, you know I can't comment on the details, Emma, but we're investigating several avenues of enquiry."

Translation: we have no idea who did this and we don't even know where to start looking.

I hid my disappointment. I had hoped the police would have made some headway by now. Instead, once again, it looked like it was going to be up to me to get to the bottom of things.

12

T he rest of the day at the Christmas Garden flew by without incident.

Before I knew it, evening had arrived, the park had closed for the night, and I found myself sitting side by side with Billy, enjoying a cup of hot cider in front of the windows facing his backyard deck. It was too cold to go out there now, like we did during the nicer weather.

I had told Billy right away about the new incident of vandalism at the park and about how Betty Blackwell had gotten so irate about it all that she'd ended up calling Tucker. I also told him how Tucker had turned up once again wearing a Santa suit.

Billy had listened attentively to my stories and laughed when I told him about Tucker's conspiratorial whisper. Now, I asked him how his day had been.

He shrugged. "Nothing glamorous. My day started with a patient's case of arthritis playing up, went downhill from there, and ended with me tending to a different patient's painful bunion."

I wrinkled my nose. Billy's job at the day clinic made my

own work as a freelance graphic designer seem much more appealing, even if my job did mean sitting up half the night, rejecting draft after draft until I hit the right design. At least there was no risk of getting sprayed with blood or pus. And no chance I'd have to deal with anyone else's feet.

My cell phone buzzed and I pulled it out of my bag. Suzy's name was on the display. Just like last time, my immediate response was to panic and think something was wrong. But then I remembered the call I took from her that morning and relaxed slightly. Apparently, calling was becoming Suzy's new favourite method of communication.

"Excuse me," I said to Billy as I took the call.

"Hey Suzy, what's up?"

"I just wanted to thank you for this morning," she replied. Her voice grew amused as she carried on. "And ask you how things are going at Billy's place."

"What? How did you know that's where I am?" I asked.

Suzy laughed. "Emma, you haven't been gone so long you've forgotten how small towns work? People see a car in somebody's driveway and they talk about it. I heard."

"It's two friends sharing cider," I said. "That's all there is to it. And seeing as you asked, it's going well."

I looked at Billy and rolled my eyes. He grinned and returned the gesture.

"Whatever. I have to go. I just wanted to check in," Suzy said. "Oh and Emma?"

"Yeah?"

"Stop being so stubborn and just date him already."

She hung up before I could respond.

13

T he next afternoon, halfway through my day's work at the Christmas Garden, I hurried across the park to catch Betty Blackwell.

I had wanted to see Betty and I hadn't been able to find her when I first arrived. I was quickly running out of time to talk to her about leaving early. Of course, as a volunteer I was free to come and go as I chose, for the most part. But having already selected the times I was free, I didn't want to just walk away without at least letting her know.

"Betty?" I shouted after her as she hurried towards the ice rink with her clipboard.

She looked over her shoulder and stopped to wait for me, not even attempting to cover her annoyance at being interrupted while she was in the middle of something.

"What is it, Emma? If there's another problem can't you just deal with it? I already have quite enough to handle. Do you know Sheriff Tucker refused to put another cop on patrol, even after all the vandalism?"

Maybe Tucker was taking Frank's murder more seriously than I had given him credit for, I thought. He had obviously stood up to Betty and refused to waste more of his man power securing an event that was hardly likely to erupt into a riot. I had to give him credit for that. Not many people dared to stand up to Betty.

"I just wanted to let you know that I have to leave early today," I said.

"How early?" Betty snapped, looking down at her clipboard as though she would find the answer there.

I checked my watch. I really had caught her in the nick of time.

"I'll be leaving in around fifteen minutes," I informed her.

I had debated asking rather than telling her, but that of course left her room to say no. I was going, whether she liked it or not.

After leaving Billy, I had spent much of my time last night thinking about the Historic Homes Christmas Tour. I was sure it would give me an answer one way or the other as to Harold Abbott's guilt.

"That's rather inconvenient, Emma," Betty commented, her acidic tone cutting through me.

I didn't like the idea of letting her and the other volunteers down, but this was a greater responsibility. Promising to get justice for a dead man had to be more important than trying to sell raffle tickets to people who really didn't want to buy them.

"Inconvenient or not, I'll still have to be leaving," I said in what I hoped was a firm but polite tone.

Betty sighed and shook her head, making no similar effort to come across as polite.

"Well then, I don't suppose I have much choice but to fill in for you myself, do I?"

I fought to keep my smile hidden. The thought of Betty

actually doing some work was a novel one, although I did feel for her prospective customers. She wasn't one to take no for an answer and I thought the people at the Christmas Garden would be likely to buy tickets if for no other reason than to get her to move on. It would be a good day for profits, I thought to myself.

"You might as well just go now," Betty snapped, holding her hand out for the ticket book.

I didn't know if it was meant to guilt me into staying, but if that had been her aim, she was way off. I handed her the ticket book, untied my money pouch from around my middle, and handed her that as well.

"Thanks, Betty. It's lovely to see you being so accommodating." I smiled.

She made a grunting sound and walked away from me.

I shrugged and headed for the marquee to collect my things. The extra fifteen minutes I'd managed to snag meant I would be able to grab a burger on the way out of the park. It wouldn't do to draw attention to myself on the home tour, and I had a feeling a rumbling stomach would do just that.

14

W hen I pulled up in front of Harold Abbott's beautiful old Victorian home, it seemed to me that it looked different than it had before. It looked darker, more threatening somehow. Maybe because this time I was actually going in there and was viewing it with an eye toward deciding whether it's owner could be a coldblooded killer.

I parked along the curb, squeezing my truck in between a line of other parked cars, presumably all visitors who had come for the tour of the historic home. After making my way up the tidy walkway between perfectly sculptured rows of shrubbery, I attached myself to the gathering group of over a dozen strangers clustered around the front porch. A male tour guide soon appeared and introduced himself. When the time was right, I showed him the ticket that Harold himself had given me, and gained admittance into the house.

While the rest of the group stood in the entryway, listening to the guide's introduction to the house and information about the family who had built it over a century ago,

I took in my surroundings. The wood panelled entry branched out in several directions leading deeper into the house. Directly ahead of our group was a twisting stairway with a beautiful hand-carved wooden railing disappearing up into the next level. Here and there, tall potted ferns brightened up the space and colorful Christmas decorations made up for the thick draperies covering the windows as if to separate the indoors and block out all signs of the outside world. I couldn't decide whether the effect of all those drapes and heavily panelled walls was smothering or cozy.

As we moved deeper into the interior, I kept an eye out for the owner of the house himself. But to my disappointment, Harold Abbott didn't make an appearance.

The tour had been going for half an hour, and so far, it wasn't so much a tour as it was a stand and listen to the lecture kind of thing. We hadn't even left the hallways yet and it seemed like the tour guide, whose name I had forgotten already, was just getting warmed up. He'd talked us through the full history of the building, which I'd mostly tuned out, and now he was going on about the age of some of the art pieces in the hall.

That was a bit more interesting, and I was listening a little more intently, but I was also getting restless. I wanted us to just move into the main body of the house so I could start to get a real feel for Harold Abbott and maybe see something incriminating. I didn't really know what I was expecting to find. It wasn't like Harold was going to have an "I killed Frank Clarkson" sign hanging up somewhere. But I believed you could tell a lot about a person by their home.

We finally started to move into the individual rooms. Our first stop was a lovely old library. The walls were lined with thick mahogany shelves filled with leather-bound books of all sizes and colors. I found myself looking around the room in awe. For a moment, I forgot about my quest and just enjoyed the papery smell of the room.

I was quickly reminded of what I was really doing there when we made to leave the library. One of the other guests on the tour pointed to a door I hadn't noticed.

"What's through there?" he asked. "I heard Mr. Abbott has an interesting collection of rare old books, including some first editions. Are we not going to be able to see those?"

"That's Mr. Abbott's private study and it's off limits to the tour, I'm afraid," the tour guide replied. "The collection you're talking about is housed in a smaller library upstairs. But don't worry. You'll have access to that."

The mention of a private study got my heart racing. If Harold Abbott had any secrets to be found, they would surely be in there. It would explain why the room was off limits. Of course, I had to bide my time. I couldn't just walk over to the room right now. I had to wait for my perfect moment.

I waited and, eventually, the moment came. The tour guide took us down a narrow passageway lined with old sepia photographs, giving us the story behind the pictures. He then led us to the end of the hall and pointed to a steep staircase, explaining that we'd next be moving upstairs, where we would see a bedroom that still possessed its original Victorian fireplace, before moving on to the rare book collection. That old book collection seemed to be the highlight of the tour.

I took my chance and fell to the back of the group, pretending to be paying close attention to one of the photographs. I waited, listening to the sound of the group moving away. Then, I started back the way we had come.

It was a large house and I figured if I was seen somewhere by Harold Abbott, I could convince him I'd hung back from the tour to look at something more closely and gotten lost. And if he happened to be in his study when I went in there, I would say I was just looking for a bathroom. It wasn't the best cover story, but he had no reason to think I was snooping around, so why shouldn't he believe me? If he had thought for a second I was poking into Frank Clarkson's murder and guessed that he was one of my main suspects, he would never have given me the ticket for the tour in the first place.

I felt a bit guilty creeping around like this when Harold had given me the ticket for free. But I reminded myself that either he was a murderer and didn't deserve my sympathy, or he was innocent, in which case he had nothing to hide. Obviously, I wasn't interested in reading his private correspondence or poking around in his accounts or anything.

I reached the library. Even though my nerves were jangling, I still couldn't help but appreciate again how lovely it was. I walked straight to the study door. I didn't know how much time I would have before the guide realized I was missing and came looking for me, so I told myself to stop hesitating and just get on with it.

Pushing the door open, I breathed a sigh of relief when I found it empty. I stepped in and closed the door quietly behind me. Glancing around the room, I looked for a suitable hiding place. Nothing I could say could get me out of this if I was discovered in here with the door closed. So if anyone came along, hiding would be my only option. The only hiding place I could see would be beneath the desk, which, in a study, would be the worst hiding spot ever, as anyone entering would likely go straight to it.

I told myself to stop messing around, get on with finding whatever it was I was looking for, and get out of there. The trouble was, I didn't really know what I was searching for. I just figured I would know it when I saw it.

I stepped further into the room. There didn't seem to be anything special or unique about the place, other than more of the same heavy wood panelling I had noted throughout the rest of the house. A potted fern stood next to a leather padded chair in the corner. It appeared potted ferns were a favourite decorative element of the home's owner.

I moved past the high-backed desk chair and my eyes quickly scanned the tidy contents arranged across the desktop. There was a computer that looked almost as antique as the house itself, a small silver clock with a swinging pendulum that filled the room with a soft ticking sound, and an old fashioned stationery set with pen, paper, and matching envelopes laid out neatly.

My gaze moved over the stationery set and was drawn to a heavy-looking glass paperweight beside it. The paperweight was a clear orb with a black swirl running through it and flecks of silver suspended permanently inside the circular prison of glass. There was something mesmerising about the way the light reflected off the glossy surface of the orb. That wasn't the reason my eyes were drawn to it, though. My attention was all for the red sticky-looking substance caked around the bottom of the orb.

My pulse raced. Was that what I thought it was? Blood? Surely not. Not lying around in the open like this. Nobody would leave something so incriminating lying where it could be easily stumbled upon. And yet, it looked very like blood...

I stepped closer, my feet taking me to the paperweight even as my mind screamed at me to just get away. I reached out to pick up the glass orb, but thought better of it. I'd watched enough crime shows to know that having your fingerprints on a potential murder weapon is never a good idea.

I reached into my purse and pulled out a plastic baggy that I always carried with me in case I had to use my umbrella on a rainy day and didn't want the umbrella dripping water everywhere after use. I turned the carrier bag inside out and wrapped it around my hand like a glove, then picked up the paperweight, folding the bag around it and slipping it into my purse.

My heart was pounding as I crept back out of the study. I hurried from the library and returned to the sepia toned photographs. Once I reached them, I turned around and stood with my back to the wall, finally allowing myself to breathe again. Pressing my head against the floral wallpaper, I closed my eyes for a moment as my racing heart slowed to a more normal rhythm.

The whole adventure had taken around seven minutes but felt like it could have been seven hours. I debated slipping away and leaving the house, but it might look suspicious if somebody noticed the missing paperweight later and started asking questions. Anyway, I had a feeling the next time I bumped into Harold Abbott he would quiz me about my thoughts on the tour. I should try and take in enough that I could answer intelligently and make myself look innocent, at least until I decided on my next step.

I hurried to the end of the passageway and up the stairs. I stopped at the top and listened. Sure enough, I could hear the tour guide's droning voice. I followed it and found the small group admiring the promised original fireplace. I had to admit it was a magnificent sight.

A hand touched my shoulder as I looked at the ornate carvings around the mantelpiece. I froze for a second, before turning slowly to meet my fate.

Fear washed over me. Maybe Harold knew where I had been and what I had taken. Was I busted? But my worries dissolved quickly when I found myself facing, not Harold Abbott, but the concerned-looking tour guide. He frowned when he saw how he had startled me.

For goodness sake, Emma, calm down, I told myself.

I forced a smile onto my lips and the guide smiled back uncertainly.

"Are you alright, Ma'am? I was just about to come looking for you. You look like you've seen a ghost."

Actually, I had seen several recently, but I knew he didn't mean it literally.

"I'm fine. I got caught up looking at the old photos downstairs. They really are fascinating, aren't they?"

The guide nodded. "They really are. There's so much history in those photographs alone," he said. "You know, copies of them are sold downtown at the news stand."

I said, "Really? I'll be sure to stop by and check them out sometime. Thanks for telling me."

Our conversation was interrupted then, when another member of the tour group called over, "What year would this fireplace have been installed?"

The tour guide turned his attention to her, leaving me alone.

I breathed a small sigh of relief. I had sensed it was only going to be a matter of time until he mentioned something specific about one of the photographs downstairs, something I wouldn't have been able to answer convincingly. Even when I'd stood staring at the pictures earlier, my mind was elsewhere and I hadn't really taken in what I was seeing.

I managed to get through the rest of the tour without drawing attention to myself, but the whole time, I was conscious of the paperweight in my possession. I felt like it was burning a hole in the bottom of my purse. I was essentially stealing it, but couldn't feel guilty for that. I'd found a blood-stained, heavy object in the house of someone who had a known grudge against a man who had been murdered with a similar blunt object. Obviously, catching a killer excused the theft of a worthless item.

When the tour was finally over, I practically ran outside. I hurried down the snowy, shrub-lined path and made my way to where the truck stood parked at the curb.

What to do next?

I considered my options, as I unlocked the truck and slid into the driver's seat.

I knew I should take the paperweight to Tucker. He was the Sheriff and any evidence should be given to him. Once I'd handed it over, it wouldn't be my problem anymore. I would have done everything I could to help the ghost of Frank Clarkson get his justice.

Except I knew that wasn't true. I didn't trust that Tucker would take me seriously enough to even test whether the blood on the paperweight matched Frank Clarkson's. He might find the connection between the two men, which mostly amounted to rumour, too tenuous to pursue. Then too, even if he were willing to listen to my suspicions, I had visions of Tucker managing to accidentally contaminate this piece of evidence so much that it would be beyond any form of usefulness.

No, I decided, I couldn't take it directly to Tucker. Not yet. So where, then?

You know exactly where, my annoyingly condescending inner voice said. *You just don't want to have to answer any questions, so you're avoiding the obvious person who could help with this.*

I nodded, admitting that inner voice was right.

I put the truck into drive and headed for Billy's place.

MINUTES LATER, I pulled into Billy's driveway and cut the engine. I got out of the truck, slammed the door, and marched up the short snow-encrusted walkway to the front door. Before I could talk myself out of it, I rang the doorbell.

As I shivered in the frosty air, it felt like forever before he came to the door.

"Emma. What a great surprise. Come on in," Billy said, stepping back to let me inside. He must have just recently gotten home from the clinic, because he was still dressed in the khaki slacks and button-down shirt he usually wore under his white coat at work.

Despite his apparent happiness to see me, I detected a question in his eyes. I didn't usually drop by unannounced like this, and he was bound to be wondering why I was doing it now.

"You might not think it's so great to see me when you find out why I'm here," I warned, as we went through to the living room.

With a concerned frown, Billy motioned for me to sit. I sat on one end of a long couch and Billy took the other end.

"So, what's going on?" he asked. "I take it something's wrong?"

I sighed. How would I even begin to explain any of it?

"I need to ask you something, Billy. And when I do, I need you to not question me. I guess I'm asking you to just trust me," I replied.

"Of course I trust you," he said, looking surprised that I would even ask. "We're still two out of the Three Musketeers, remember? If something's wrong, you can always come to me."

I nodded. I had expected nothing less.

Retrieving the plastic baggy from my purse, I held it out to him.

"Don't touch what's inside. There may be fingerprints or DNA we don't want to contaminate," I cautioned him.

He frowned, peering into the bag, but was careful not to touch the paperweight.

"You've probably got all kinds of fancy equipment down at the clinic, right?" I asked. "Can you test the blood on the bottom of this paperweight and identify who it belongs to?"

His brows drew even further together at the mention of blood and he ran a hand through his hair. "Well, sure, we can test it, but not at the local clinic. I'd have to send a sample off to the lab and the results would take a couple days to come through. Anyway, what are you up to, Emma? Where did this thing come from?"

"You promised not to ask questions," I reminded him.

"I know, but I would need to know what results we're looking for," he said.

Then, as I tried to decide how much to tell him, he saved me the trouble. Looking more closely at the paperweight in its baggy, he said, "Anyway, I think I can save us the trouble of testing this."

"How so?"

"Because that's not blood on the bottom of the paperweight."

"What?"

"It's something else. Looks like red ink maybe. At any rate, I'm familiar with the sight of old blood and this definitely isn't it," Billy said.

I ground my teeth in disappointment. How had I made such a rookie mistake? And in front of Billy, too.

It suddenly occurred to me that I valued Billy's opinion of my intelligence much more than I cared to admit. Now was not the time for that revelation, but there it was, all the same.

I couldn't see where to go from here, and I knew the questions would start now, for sure. To prevent that, I jumped to my feet and took the bag out of Billy's hands.

"Okay, thank you. I'm sorry to have bothered you," I garbled out, as I hurried for the door.

Billy got up and followed me.

"You didn't bother me, Emma. But I would like to know what's going on with all this talk of blood and fingerprints," he said. "Just tell me, are you in some kind of trouble?

I tried to look innocent. "Who? Me? Nope, no trouble at all. Everything's peachy, but now I have to go."

As I twisted the front door handle, I didn't give him another chance to speak. "Catch you later. Thanks, Billy." I said in a rush, and then I was gone.

I hurried back to the truck and pulled out of the driveway, knowing full well that Billy was calling after me. There was no way I was sticking around to tell him the truth about how I was seeking justice for a ghost.

Sure, he knew I had ghostly visions. But he didn't know they were real spirits, not just the product of a head injury, or that I did the ghosts' bidding. I didn't want him thinking I was nuts, but I didn't want to lie to him either. So getting out of there as fast as I could had been the only solution.

Once I was clear of Billy's house, I pulled over onto the shoulder alongside the road and put the offending paperweight, still in the carrier bag, back into my purse. I was now a thief for nothing. It seemed that Harold Abbott was innocent after all. Which lead me back to Frank Clarkson's killer being either Betty Blackwell or the mysterious woman in the green coat.

Neither of those options really seemed right to me. Deep down, I thought Betty was harmless, even if a little rude. And the woman in the green coat was so elusive I could almost believe I had imagined her.

My cell phone buzzed and I pulled it out to see a text message from Billy. Quickly, I texted back.

BILLY: Talk 2 me. Let me help U.

ME: Promise I'll explain later.

BILLY: I'll hold U 2 that.

I COULDN'T HELP but smile as I put the truck back into gear and headed home. Maybe Suzy was right and I should stop getting in my own way and just give Billy a real chance. It was something to think about.

By the time I got home, night had well and truly fallen. Grandma and Grandpa were already in bed, but I didn't return to a completely still house. Snowball charged at me the second I came through the door, her cute little bleat sounding so happy to see me that it made me laugh in spite of everything. I knelt down and fussed the little goat.

"Oh, Snowball, whatever have I gotten myself into with this one?" I whispered.

She bleated wisely, but the meaning was somewhat lost. I took comfort from stroking her soft fur, instead.

Still, my mind was turning over the same old question. If the killer wasn't Harold Abbott, and it wasn't Betty Blackwell, and it wasn't the woman in the green coat, then who was it? And how was I meant to go about working it all out?

"Come on, girl. I have an idea," I told Snowball, standing back up.

I headed through the kitchen and out the back door, wondering all the time if I was actually crazy for thinking this could work. I passed the outhouse and went to stand behind it so that if either of my grandparents happened to look out their bedroom window, they wouldn't see me. If they saw a flash of Snowball, they would simply assume I was using the outhouse and she was waiting for me, like she had done hundreds of times before.

"Frank? Are you here? Can you hear me?" I whispered.

I got nothing in return.

Snowball remained standing, rubbing herself against my legs like an affectionate cat. She always made a hasty retreat to a safe distance when I was about to get a spooky visitor, so her presence now was a sign there was no ghost around.

I tried again. "Please, Frank. If you can hear me, come out and talk. Tell me where to start. I'm seriously trying my best here, but I'm no further forward than Tucker, and that's not a good thing to have to admit."

Again there was nothing.

I gave up. Angrily, I went into the outhouse to do my business, slamming the door behind me. I could still hear Snowball's bleating outside, but it didn't sound alarmed or excited, like she was trying to tell me I had a ghostly visitor. Once more, it was clear that I was in this alone.

I finished up and left the outhouse, heading back for the farmhouse. By the time I reached the bottom of the stairs to the back porch and climbed them quietly, Snowball was hot on my heels.

Indoors, the goat followed me up to my room, where she promptly grabbed one of my socks and began nibbling on it.

I shook my head, more amused than annoyed. There was something comical about a little white goat with a pink sock in its mouth.

"I allow you up here to be nice and this is how you repay me?" I teased her, as I huddled on my bed and fired up my laptop.

I was going to do some more work on Eva's design project, and I wasn't going to let myself be distracted. Not by thoughts of Frank Clarkson, Harold Abbott, Betty Blackwell, the green-coated woman, or even Billy.

15

The snow was falling again, thickening up the blanket of white spread over Hollow Heights Park and the Christmas Garden. I wore a thick coat, a hat and scarf, and woolly gloves, and I was still freezing.

I pushed my sleeves down, pulling my hands inside them, bouncing on my toes, trying anything to keep the blood flowing. My breath plumed in front of me, a cloud of white that I could imagine falling to the ground as frozen fragments of ice.

At least, being so cold helped to stop me from thinking about last night, although the topic still weighed heavily on my mind. I kept remembering how I had run out on Billy, how he must think I had completely lost it.

Maybe I had. After all, who mistook red ink for blood? I worried that I was getting as bad as Tucker. I had wanted a neat, easy solution, so I had made a connection where there wasn't one, just like Tucker had when he thought Frank Clarkson had been killed by a reindeer's kick.

"Emma? Are you listening?" Ruth, one of the fair volunteers, smiled.

Okay, maybe the cold wasn't pulling me out of my thoughts quite enough.

"I'm sorry. I was a million miles away. What were you saying?" I asked.

"I was asking who the lucky guy is," Ruth grinned, flashing a row of perfect white teeth.

"What lucky guy?"

"Oh, come on. You've been distracted all day. You must have someone on your mind," she teased, tucking a strand of long dark hair behind her ear. She was a friendly woman a few years younger than me, just the right age to want to exchange a little romantic gossip.

Unfortunately, that was the last topic I wanted to entertain right now.

"There's no guy, lucky or otherwise. I was just thinking about what to get my grandpa for Christmas," I lied.

It wasn't like Billy would come anywhere near me now, I told myself. Not after the weird way I had acted last night.

The idea of Billy finally giving up on me made me strangely sad. Like, really sad. Like, sad where I actually wanted to bawl my eyes out and eat ice cream.

"Oh, well, there's an easy answer to that," Ruth replied, her thoughts obviously following a different track than mine. "Just ask your grandma. She'll know what your grandpa wants for Christmas."

"Yeah, I reckon you're right about that one," I said.

"Speak of the devil," Ruth said.

She nodded into the crowd and I spotted my grandma and a few of her quilting circle friends heading straight for us.

"You can ask her now."

"Oh no, don't mention it to her right now. Her friends

will all have an opinion on it, and it could get ugly." I laughed.

I'd had Grandpa's present in for weeks now and Grandma knew it. I had of course gone to her already for her advice and if Ruth said anything now, Grandma would know there was something else going on here. I really didn't want to have to fend off a list of questions that would end in me once more lying to her.

"I'm telling you, this town is going to the dogs," Ethel said as Grandma and her crowd moved into earshot.

"That's a bit extreme," my grandma told her.

"Is it? Multiple murders this past year, cases of vandalism in the park, and now this. I mean, what's next?"

Grandma ignored her and turned to me instead.

"Hi Emma. How's it going?" she asked me. "Have you sold many tickets for the big raffle?"

The big raffle, as it was jokingly known, was to win the fair's star prize: a homemade Christmas cake. The raffle tradition had started two years ago apparently, and although every woman in town seemed to be of the opinion that their own cake recipes were far superior to the one Mrs Beale made for the prize, everyone still wanted a ticket or two or five.

"Yes." I smiled. "Almost three hundred and counting."

"I've got mine." Grandma beamed. "Maybe if I win, I'll share my secret with Mrs Beale, so I can have a delicious cake with no effort."

"It'll probably be poisoned, the way things are going," Ethel mumbled.

I thought of what she had been saying when she approached us.

"What's happened now?" I asked Ethel.

"What do you mean, dear?" she asked.

"When you came over, you said the town was going to the dogs because of all the murder and the vandalism and then you said *and now this*," I reminded her.

"Oh, of course. Yes. There's been a burglary," Ethel announced.

I could hear the glee in her voice as she said it. Going to the dogs or not, Ethel for one was loving all of the drama.

"A burglary?" I prompted, as Grandma snorted with derision.

"Yes. Harold Abbott was robbed."

"Nonsense," Grandma put in. "He's just being dramatic, as always."

"He claims to have had an expensive paperweight, an antique or something, stolen during one of the tours of his house," Rose clarified.

I felt horror flood through me as the color rushed to my face. It hadn't even occurred to me that the paperweight could have any material value.

"I'm telling you, he's moved the thing and forgotten where he's put it. And now that he's caused so much of a scene, he's sticking to his story to save face," Diane said.

I couldn't tell them that Harold hadn't in fact misplaced the paperweight. That it was sitting in my purse in the marquee. I was suddenly glad of the bitter cold. It meant that my cheeks would already be flushed enough that none of the ladies would see my blush of embarrassment.

"He even called Tucker," Grandma said.

I was suddenly relieved that Tucker wasn't exactly Sherlock Holmes.

"So who does Mr. Abbott suspect?" I asked.

I was almost afraid to hear the answer, but I figured that

if he had been telling people he had an inkling it was me, Grandma would have mentioned it before now.

"That's what makes it all so ridiculous," Margene put in. "He doesn't even remember the exact time he last saw it, so even if it had been taken, that's a full week of tours, twice daily with up to twenty people on each one. How would anyone even start to work out exactly who had taken the thing?"

"I guess they'll have to wait and see if it turns up at the local pawn shop," I mused.

"It won't. It'll turn up somewhere in the house and Harold will casually drop the case. I swear he's going senile," Rose said.

I cringed inside. The last thing I had wanted to do was draw attention to any of this, and I certainly didn't like the idea of making a man question his sanity. Yet it seemed that was exactly what I had done.

I knew then that I had to find a way to get the paper-weight back into Harold Abbott's house. Ideally, I needed to plant it somewhere close enough to the study desk that it would be plausible that it had been knocked to the ground and rolled there. That way Harold wouldn't be forced to question his sanity. And the paperweight would still be far enough away that no one would wonder why it wasn't spotted sooner.

This whole thing had been much easier when I was almost sure Harold was the killer. Now that it had all proved to be a complicated waste of time, part of me thought I never should have promised Frank Clarkson's ghost that I would do any of this. Things were getting much too difficult.

Grandma and the others were debating amongst them-selves whether or not they believed Harold Abbott had really been robbed. None of them seemed to have noticed my sudden silence, which was good.

"Come on," Rose said, "let's go and get some apple cider."

The others muttered their agreement and I was relieved they would be leaving me alone with my thoughts for a moment. I almost wished they hadn't told me about the assumed burglary. But in another sense, I was glad they had. Now that I knew the paperweight was worth something, I understood I had to return it instead of finding somewhere to dump it, as I had been planning. I had only held onto it this long in case Billy had called and asked to take another look at it.

But of course Billy hadn't called. Or texted. He was clearly avoiding the crazy girl. Who could blame him?

"Emma, would you do me a favor and call in to the dry cleaners on your way home? My Christmas blouse should be ready," Grandma said.

I nodded.

"Yes, of course, Grandma. Do you have the ticket?"

"Just give her my name," Grandma said.

She looked at me like it was crazy to assume someone would need any sort of a receipt to prove their things actually belonged to them.

Grandma and the others wandered away. They were already arguing about the exact right amount of sugar to put in Christmas cookies. For such good friends, those women couldn't agree on any single thing.

I turned my mind back to my Harold Abbott problem. The answer was pretty simple. I would have to go on another tour of his house and return the paperweight in the same way I'd taken it. I doubted my errand would be as easy this time, though. Harold probably had his study locked now. But as I considered it, a plan began to form in my head.

I would attempt to get the item into his study, but if the door was locked, I would leave the paperweight somewhere along the tour. As long as I was careful not to be seen, it would work all round. Harold would get his paperweight back, and with it, his dignity. If the thing was found on the tour route, it would look like he had been right all along and that the guilty party had become remorseful and returned the paperweight.

I pulled my cell phone out and scrolled through my call list until I found the call I'd made to the ticket booking line the other day. I quickly connected the call, and within five minutes, I had a ticket reserved for that night's tour.

That was the easy part done. Now came the harder part: telling Betty Blackwell I had to leave early again.

I would need to leave within the next half an hour if I was to get Grandma's blouse from the dry cleaners and still make the tour on time. I knew Betty wasn't going to like it, and even though she had no real say over whether or not I would be able to leave, I felt guilty for letting her down two days in a row.

I went to seek her out before I could change my mind.

I headed for the marquee and was pleased to find her there. At least she was warm and dry, so her mood would be slightly better than it would be if she was outside in the biting wind and snow.

"Betty, I'm just letting you know I'll be leaving at three today," I said as I approached her.

"The youth of today have no work ethic anymore," she muttered. "Well, the youth and Frank Clarkson."

I ignored the jibe. "I'm sorry. Really, I am. But it's for my grandma," I said.

It wasn't an entire lie; I did need to go to the dry cleaners for Grandma, but I injected just enough of an edge into my voice that implied it was something more serious than that.

I felt a little guilty when Betty's face softened and she nodded.

"Of course, yes, do whatever you need to do, Emma," she said.

I knew what I'd said would make it easier all around, and that it was the only way to get away early without there being a big scene, but it didn't stop me from feeling bad for using Grandma as an excuse.

"Thank you," I said.

"No worries. Dorothy is a lovely woman who has done a lot for this town and if she needs something, of course she should come first. Emma, I'm sorry for comparing you to Frank. You're nothing like him. Or, indeed, like the lazy youth. I know you do a lot for your grandparents."

I wasn't expecting that and it threw me for a second. I smiled and nodded at Betty. I thought about her reference to Frank and decided to take my chances on getting her to talk while she was being particularly open and decidedly un-Betty like.

"What exactly did Frank Clarkson do?" I asked.

"As little as he possibly could," Betty replied. "That man would never work a full day if he thought he could get away with half of one."

"But he volunteered his time for the Christmas Garden," I reminded her. "So he can't have been all bad."

"Look, Emma, I don't want to speak ill of the dead, but that man was no good."

"You were arguing with him, weren't you, on your first day here?" I asked. I made a show of trying to remember the exact details, as if they weren't engraved on my memory. "It was not long before ... well, you know. Had he tried to shirk some responsibility or another?"

"No, nothing like that. That much I would have expected. What he did was worse."

She looked from side to side, as if to make sure we weren't being over heard.

"I caught him being cruel to the reindeer. He was yelling at one and hitting it with a stick. I know people think I'm pretty hard hearted, and I guess I don't have a high tolerance level for idiots. But I do have a lot of feeling for animals. And those innocent creatures deserved better. Anyway, I told him I was going to dismiss him as soon as I found a new reindeer wrangler. He started yelling at me. I wasn't about to stand there and take that, as I'm sure you can imagine."

I smiled. I could well imagine.

"Now all of that is water under the bridge, of course," she continued. "Frank is gone and there's no need to spread unpleasant truths about the dead. Anyway, you run along, Emma. I don't want to make you late. And if you need any more time off, just let me know and I can arrange something."

"Thank you, but that won't be necessary. You've already been more than fair," I admitted.

I collected my purse, with the offending paperweight still inside it, and headed for the parking lot. I had seen a very different side to Betty Blackwell during our conversation, one I hadn't known she'd possessed. If someone had told me she had a softer side, I would have thought they were imagining it. But now that I'd seen it with my own eyes, I wasn't sure what to make of it.

On one hand, Betty wasn't the cold-hearted person I had her down as, and it made her a lot less likely as a murder suspect. On the other hand, what if she was inventing the whole reindeer story to throw me and anyone else off the scent, hiding some real, deeper quarrel with Frank?

This case was getting more complex by the day. I was starting to think I would fail to come through on my promise to Frank's ghost.

16

M y nerves had already kicked in by the time I reached Harold Abbott's house.

Before I went to register for the tour, I took a moment to compose myself and to try and look like I wasn't there for anything except some interesting history. I sat in my grandpa's truck, peering out the window at the falling snow, trying to convince myself everything would be fine.

My worry about potentially getting caught was different this time. When I'd been here before, I'd been afraid that if I was seen snooping I'd have to come up with something that could explain my presence in an off-limits part of the house. Then, I'd been worried about how to hide the fact that I had considered Harold a murder suspect.

Now, I returned out of my own guilt, concerned about being discovered with a stolen article in my possession.

Although I was still nervous about what I had to do as I clambered out of the truck and hurried through the snow, I told myself it shouldn't be too hard to hide the paperweight somewhere along the tour route. I'd finally settled on that idea as much simpler than trying to smuggle the object back into the study. With any luck, when Harold found the paperweight, he would just be pleased that whoever had taken it had brought it back. There was no way the theft could be tied to me as long as I wasn't caught returning it.

I felt a flood of relief when I saw that the tour guide this time was different from the last one. It would have been harder to hang back and not draw attention to myself if it was the same guide who would remember me from before.

I was one of the first people to arrive for the tour.

"Hi. I'm Kelly," the pretty tour guide said with a smile.

"Emma," I replied.

Instantly, I could have bit my tongue. I really didn't want her to know who I was. I hoped to straggle behind the group a little and not interact much at all. Introducing myself to the guide wasn't the best start to my plan.

"Have you always been interested in history, Emma?" Kelly asked me.

I thought quickly and inspiration for how I could make this play out to my advantage hit me. I wasn't certain it would work, but I knew it could if I managed it just right.

"I do enjoy learning about history, but I have to confess to having an ulterior motive for coming on the tour," I said.

Kelly looked at me, a question written all over her face.

"I've been on the tour before," I admitted. "I got so caught up looking at the antique photos in the hallway that I kind of missed a lot of the tour. And my main passion is old books, so I really wanted to come back and have a good look at the books in Harold's collection."

"You know Mr. Abbott personally?" Kelly asked.

It had worked. I cheered inside.

"Oh, yes. He and my grandparents go way back," I said.

It wasn't a total lie. Most people in this town "went way

back". And I didn't say they were close, I just implied it. I had laid the foundation that might allow me to hang back in the book collection room. I had also given Kelly a possible reason to feel comfortable with leaving me there alone.

"It must be lovely living in a town with such a community feel," Kelly said. "I grew up in a big city and my family never had much of a relationship with our neighbours."

"It's great the way everyone knows one another," I agreed. "But it has its down sides too. Like how everyone knows your business."

I leaned in closer to her as other tour members started to arrive.

"And the bits they don't know, they just make up."

Kelly laughed.

More people had arrived now and a quick count told me this group was about the same size as the last one.

Kelly confirmed my suspicions by clapping her hands together loudly. "Okay, everyone, let's get started," she said in a voice full of cheer.

She turned around, we followed her into the house, and the tour began.

I couldn't help but glance at Harold's study door as we looked around the first library. I had to fight a sudden urge to try the handle, just to see if the door was locked now. No one in the group asked anything about the closed door, and I was glad. If they had, I might have ended up blushing or something equally bad and given myself away somehow.

As we passed the sepia photographs in the next hallway, I made a point of glancing at each one long enough to have an opinion on it so that if Kelly asked me anything about them, I would have an answer. She didn't ask, but I was glad I'd taken the time to look at them properly this time. They really were interesting. Besides, any potential problem I could eliminate brought my stress levels down a notch. That could only be a good thing.

We made our way up the stairs and into the room with the Victorian fireplace.

I actually got interested in the historical information Kelly was giving out, and some of the other people on the tour asked good questions that pulled me in even further. By the time we left the room, I could almost pretend that I was just another history buff on a tour of a historical home. Almost, but not quite.

My palms were sweating and my heart was beating a little faster than it should. I could still feel the paperweight almost burning a hole in my purse, and the faster I got rid of the thing, the better. I still couldn't quite believe I had managed to take something old and valuable. I would make a terrible thief, because to me it looked like a standard paperweight from any office supply chain.

The tour continued and I tried to lose myself again in the information Kelly was presenting, but I couldn't. My mind was stuck firmly on what I had to do next and my pounding heart wouldn't let me forget it.

By the time we reached the room holding the collection of rare or early edition books, my mouth was dry and my palms were moist – a perfect reversal of the way they were meant to be.

We entered the room, a small chamber containing more of the typical wood panelling and thick drapes over the windows. Striped green and burgundy colored wallpaper ran up and down the walls, making me feel vaguely dizzy.

Despite my nervousness, I was once more taken aback by the size of the book collection. The whole room held countless hidden gems that were worth a fortune, yes, but they held so much more than monetary value. It was like a slice of history right there in front of me, tangible history I could hold in my hands.

Kelly talked for a moment and then, with a cheery bounce in her step, lead the group back to the door. I hung back and Kelly, more efficient than the last tour guide, looked at me questioningly as I made a point of studying the books. I turned to her with a smile.

"It's so amazing to see these works preserved so well for the next generation, isn't it?" I asked.

Kelly nodded. Her smile didn't slip as I moved on to the next book, staring at the spine as though I was taking in every detail. But I saw from the corner of my eye that she was subtly glancing at her watch. She was probably due to finish work within the next few minutes. My hanging back this way was slowing her down.

"You go on. I don't want to hold everyone up. I'll be downstairs in a minute," I said.

"Umm, Mr. Abbott isn't too keen on having people left unattended," she replied.

I pretended not to hear, and continued to examine the books.

"An old edition of Little Women." I smiled, nodding towards the book on the shelf. "Imagine the joy a book like that brings."

Kelly didn't respond. She was looking from me to the hallway and I realized that more than half of the group had wandered off. It was now or never. I had to remind Kelly that Harold Abbott was a family friend and make her feel comfortable leaving me behind.

I said, "I'll have to remember to ask Harold sometime how he came by such a precious book. I'm sure I remember him saying he inherited it from an aunt. Who was it again?" I pretended to think for a moment. "Oh, that's right. It was

Aunt Claire. Did you ever meet her? What a character she was."

"I didn't realize you and Mr. Abbott were so close," Kelly commented.

It was working. I could see it in her eyes. She wanted to be able to justify leaving me behind.

"Oh, sure. The Abbotts would come to my grandparents' on Christmas Eve for dinner and we would go to them on New Year's Eve. Of course, we saw each other at other times too, but those dates were set in stone. No matter what was going on in our lives, those get togethers would always happen."

Kelly nodded impatiently and then lowered her voice.

"Look, I know this is kind of unprofessional, but you obviously know your way around here. I have to go and catch up with others; some of them have wandered away. You'll catch us up, right?"

I nodded.

"Sure. Don't let me hold you up. I shouldn't be too long. Harold mentioned a very old copy of Alice's Adventures in Wonderland and I just want to get a quick glimpse of it."

Kelly hurried away while I was still talking and I smiled to myself. That had gone well. Better than I had hoped . I gave her a couple of minutes to be sure she was well away from the room and then I began to look around.

Other than the bookshelves, there wasn't a lot to the room, but there was a small table of framed photos in one corner. I debated leaving the paperweight on the table, but I knew Harold would never believe it had been there all along without him spotting it, so I settled on placing it under the table. I made a silent apology to his housekeeper in my head. When the item was discovered there, it would seem like she had done very little to clean the floor in this room.

I made my way over to the table and opened my purse. I pulled out the plastic bag containing the paperweight and gently rolled the glass orb out onto the floor. Then I returned the bag, empty now, to my purse.

When I stood up, I was smiling to myself. I had done it. I'd gotten away with it. Even if someone came in here now, they would never suspect I had stolen the paperweight and then returned it. I might have exaggerated Harold Abbot's relationship with my grandparents, but they had enough mutual respect for each other that Harold would never suspect their granddaughter would be behind something so terrible. Or, at least I hoped that was true.

I hurried out from behind the table and rushed across the room, planning to catch up with the tour group. Too late, I felt the toe of my shoe catch in one of the tassels of a small rug that lay beside the table.

I went sprawling, hitting the floor with a loud crash.

Great. I might not draw attention to myself as a thief, but it seemed I might attract plenty of attention as a klutz. I got back to my feet and rubbed my scraped knees. The rug had done little to cushion my fall across the hardwood floor.

I dusted myself off and turned around to straighten the rug back up. That was when I saw it. At first, I didn't know what I was looking at. I only knew that the patch of floor I had accidentally uncovered looked different than the rest. I frowned and peered at the boards, forgetting for a moment that I was in a hurry to get out of there. The strange patch of flooring explained why a rug had been placed in such a weird position. I guessed Harold had noticed a fault in the wood and wanted to hide it. There was a square beneath the rug that was going in the opposite direction to the rest of the boards. Where the others ran east to west in the rest of the room, that square ran north to south.

That didn't make sense, I thought to myself. Someone as house proud as Harold would never have accepted shoddy workmanship and covered it with a rug. He would have insisted on whatever carpenter had fitted this flooring fixing the mistake. I stepped closer and noticed a tiny, narrow gap around the oddly placed boards.

Curiosity getting the better of me, I knelt down for a closer look, wincing at the stinging pain in my grazed knees as I put my weight on them. The tiny, almost invisible thumb space I was looking at wasn't a mistake. It was some sort of hatch.

I slipped my thumb into the gap. The square of floor opened easily. As I lifted it, I fantasized about the secret passageway I might find beneath it and where it would lead to. I had read enough detective books as a youngster to know that old houses like this had a tendency towards secret passageways, hidden rooms and fake walls.

But what greeted me wasn't a secret passageway. It was much more chilling than that.

It was a small space, not even big enough for a toddler to sit in. Judging by the cobwebs inside, it was an ancient fixture of the house, maybe a cubby for hiding money or jewellery. But there wasn't money or jewellery down there now.

In the centre of the hiding spot was a single item—a brick. The original orange color of the brick was intact at one end, but the other end told the story of why the item was hidden in the floor. It was stained red with a dried, sticky-looking substance. Instinctively, I sensed this time I wasn't looking at ink. I knew in that moment that I was looking at the real murder weapon used to kill Frank Clarkson.

A cold sweat breaking out on my forehead, I tried to

think fast. Quickly, I opened my purse and got my plastic bag out again. I picked the brick up and dropped it into the bag and slipped that inside my purse.

I scrambled to my feet and began to pull the rug back into place, even as I heard footsteps from the hall approaching the doorway.

Calm down, I told myself. *It's just the tour guide coming back for you. Play it cool.*

I whirled around so my back was to the door, as if I was looking at the book collection again. I was just in the nick of time. A squeal of hinges announced the opening of the door.

"Well, who have we here? Emma Hooper, isn't it?" Harold Abbott asked from the doorway.

My heart sped up, pounding so hard and so fast I felt certain he would hear it.

Play it cool. He has no reason to suspect anything, I told myself.

I turned towards him with what I hoped was a charming smile. "Hi, Mr. Abbott. I'm sorry, I was so fascinated by these books, I just had to stay back a moment and really take them in. How many do you have now?" I asked.

I was babbling and I knew it.

Harold smiled. "One less than you seem to think," he replied

My brows drew together. "What do you mean?"

"According to the tour guide, you seem to be under the impression I've got a very old copy of Alice's Adventures in Wonderland in my collection. I assure you that is not the case. I can't help but wonder why you would assert such a thing."

He stepped into the room and closed the door behind him.

As I heard the soft double click sound of the door shutting, I could feel the panic building within me. His tone had been soft and deliberate, with a frightening edge of malice. How could I answer his question?

"You didn't recently get that book?" I asked, knowing my voice sounded too cheery. "I must have gotten you mixed up with someone else."

I took a step forward but Harold stood in the centre of the room, blocking my escape route. As I came forward, he made no attempt to move. I stopped, offering a questioning smile.

He said, "I don't think that's true, Emma. You're an intelligent woman. You would know the value of such a rare book, and you wouldn't forget who you had that sort of conversation with."

"Why would I lie about something like that?" I asked, hoping to gauge exactly how much he knew.

"To throw the tour guide off the scent of your misdeeds. This is the second time you've been here. And to think last time I gave you a free ticket, and you thanked me by stealing an expensive paperweight. And now, you're trying to steal one of these books. I hate to make such an accusation of Ed and Dorothy Hooper's granddaughter, and prior to tonight I would never have suspected you."

I felt my jaw drop. He didn't know what I was doing here or what I had found. He believed me to be nothing but a thief. Maybe this could work to my advantage. Maybe he had called the police to report me. Maybe he had Tucker already on his way here. Once I was arrested, I could show Tucker the brick and explain everything.

I looked down at the ground, purposely fiddling with my hands folded in front of me. "I don't know what you're talking about," I said, in a way that made it sound like I knew exactly what he was talking about. "How can you accuse me of such a terrible thing?"

He smiled, an almost gentle expression.

"I understand your situation, Emma. Running a farm isn't what it used to be. The money just isn't there anymore. And you don't have a real job in town. But you wanted to contribute, to help your grandparents out. And for that reason, I'm not going to report you. I know what it would do to your grandparents to see you arrested for theft. Just give me back whichever valuable book you've slipped into your purse, return the paperweight, and leave. We'll say no more about it."

I hated the pity in his voice, the way he assumed my grandparents were struggling so much that I had resorted to something like this. I had to remind myself not to indignantly tell him that the farm was extremely profitable because it was run well, and what was more, I had a "real" job in freelance design. But it was better if he thought me a desperate thief than a snoop who had discovered his dark secret.

Still, I couldn't open my purse in front of him.

"I don't have any book," I said.

"A likely story," Harold replied.

He moved closer and I took a step back. He looked pointedly at my purse and held his hand out.

I clutched the purse to me tightly, shaking my head.

Harold sighed. "Come now, Emma. If you haven't taken one of my books, prove it. Let me see inside your purse. If I'm wrong, I will sincerely apologise and hope you can forgive me."

"I'm not showing you anything," I insisted.

I moved along the wall, trying to put more distance between Harold and me. As he came closer, I realized my mistake too late. By making him follow me along the wall, I had inadvertently put him in line to see the rug beside the table. The rug that was still askew, revealing a small part of the trap door.

"Yes, that's another thing," I said, trying to get in with an accusation before he could speak. "I tripped over that stupid rug and hurt my knees pretty badly. I should sue you."

Harold looked from the rug to my face.

I saw by the look in his eyes that my ruse was over. He knew I had found the bloody brick. The sudden panic crossing his face said he also knew that I recognized exactly what it was—a murder weapon.

His brief flash of panic disappeared quickly, to be replaced by an unnerving look of confidence, as we stood watching each other. Our eyes locked, neither of us wanting to look away first. He surprised me by smiling, amusement dancing in his eyes.

"I see that I was wrong in my hasty assumptions. You weren't in here scoping out my books. You were here to snoop for something else. And then you happened upon my little secret. I suppose you've already slipped the evidence into your purse, judging by how tightly you're gripping it."

I shrugged, not exactly confirming the truth of his statement, but not denying it either. It was too late for a denial. He knew as well as I did that he was right.

"That's a shame," he said. "You see, if you were just a dirty little thief, I would have kept my word not to speak of it, protecting your grandparents' reputation. But it seems you've had no such compassion for me."

"Murder is a bit more serious than stealing a paperweight," I said.

"Indeed it is. And that's one of the reasons I can't have this getting out."

His smile was a strange mixture of sadness and glee, a look that made me wither inside. I knew then that he had no intention of letting me leave this room alive.

I had one hope and one hope only. I had to keep him talking. Maybe if I stalled long enough, a miracle would happen. Maybe the tour guide would come back to look for me. Maybe some of the other tourists would stumble onto the scene.

"Tell me why," I asked, hoping to prolong the conversation.

"Why what?" he replied.

"Why did you kill Frank Clarkson? I mean, I know you weren't exactly best friends, but you were neighbours. You'd known each other a long time."

"He sullied the memory of my wife," Harold snapped, emotion clouding his face.

He took a deep breath and ran a hand through his thinning hair.

When he spoke again, his voice was closer to normal. "For years Frank lowered the tone of our properties. His home was a disgrace, and the lawn and garden were even worse. When my wife died, I wanted this house and the garden she had loved to be a tribute to her memory. I thought Frank would respect that. Instead, he got angry and refused to clean up his place. I complained regularly over the years, but it seemed he was determined to antagonize me. Everything came to a head this past month. The day my sign went up advertising the historic tour, Frank dragged an old bathtub and toilet out onto his lawn. He placed them as close to my land as he could, clearly intending to provoke me."

"Why didn't you build a fence?" I asked, genuinely

curious as to why Harold hadn't just separated the two yards.

"I applied for planning permission but it was turned down. Some nonsense about ruining the architectural integrity of the properties. Ridiculous. How could a fence be an issue when Frank's junk wasn't? Anyway, the bathroom suite was a step too far. I gave Frank a deadline to have the thing cleared and, when he didn't comply, I went to the Christmas Fair where he was working to confront him."

I had an idea where this was heading, but I didn't interrupt.

"I found him in the reindeer pen and demanded to know when the bathtub and toilet would be removed. He told me they'd be moved when he was ready to move them. His smug smirk was enraging. I knew the argument was getting out of hand, so I tried to do the sensible thing. I turned and began to walk away. But then, Frank called after me. He stood with his back to me, while he refilled one of the reindeer troughs. He called back that I was wasting my time on my home and garden, that my wife was too dead to know the difference."

Harold's face had grown alarmingly red as he recounted his story. Now there was something more than anger in his expression. There was pain.

He continued, "Frank told me my wife was rotting in the ground. Gone. I snapped then. Something gripped me. A wild anger like nothing I had ever seen or felt before."

Harold's moment of weakness fled and his voice hardened at the memory.

"I let myself into the pen, scooped up an old brick lying on the ground, and ran towards Frank. He never saw it coming. I smashed the brick into his skull and he fell to the ground. I hadn't meant to kill him; I only wanted to shut him up. When I saw I'd done far more than that, I panicked. I opened the gate, shooing the reindeer out, hoping to cause enough chaos to sneak away. I got out of there without being seen. I didn't even realize until I was away from the scene that I still clutched the murder weapon in my hand, the bloody brick that could incriminate me. Luckily, I knew where I could hide it until talk of Frank's death died away, at which point, I could get rid of it. I knew Sheriff Tucker would never work out what had happened or that it was me who killed Frank. I decided to get on with my life. It was working too, until you came along. A typical busy body, poking your nose into things you don't understand."

He took a step closer.

Already pressed against the wall, I had no room left to back up. I threw a desperate glance at the door, wondering if I should shout for help. I had no idea how far away the tour guide and the rest of the group would be. If they didn't hear me I was doomed, because my shouting would surely make Harold act quicker. He was getting on in years, it was true, but he still looked fit enough that I didn't like my chances if it came to a physical struggle. I also had no way of knowing whether he had any sort of weapon that he might use against me in this room.

Harold saw me looking longingly at the door. He laughed.

"No one is coming, Emma. The tour is long over and everyone has left. I told the tour guide that I would indulge you personally, you know, being that our families are so close."

His sarcasm wasn't lost on me. I bit my tongue to stop myself from saying something back.

"The cheery Kelly was only too pleased to get away," Harold added. "So it's just you and me now."

He took another step towards me. He might have killed Frank in a flash of temper, but clearly he had no problem killing me in a colder, more thought out fashion just to shut me up.

There was only one thing for it, I realized. I would have to fight to escape. I did, after all, have a brick in my purse—one that had already proved itself to be an efficient tool for killing.

Still, I tried to think of something less risky. Harold was still a couple yards away from me. The space wasn't very big, but if I could get around him I was confident I could outrun him. Only he had nothing to lose at this point, and he would do whatever it took to stop me getting past him.

A terrifying plan formed in my mind, one that required me to keep him talking and distracted.

I said, "Look, let's be rational here. You don't want to kill me. Unlike with Frank, you don't have any grudge against me."

Harold smirked. "And I'm guessing your next line will be a promise not to turn me in to the police?"

Obviously, he wasn't going to fall for that line.

"No. In fact, I was going to suggest the opposite. I think you should go to Sheriff Tucker and tell him what you told me. That you didn't mean to kill Frank. The fight just got out of hand."

Harold started to shake his head.

I knew I had to make my move now, if I was to have any chance of pulling it off. I ran left, heading for the door, even as I threw my purse at Harold. He saw the heavy bag coming quickly enough to move aside and prevent it from hitting him square in the face like I had planned. But he didn't dodge fast enough to avoid being struck altogether. My purse, weighted by the brick inside it, smacked Harold in the shoulder. Thrown off balance by the unexpected blow, he stumbled backward, over the edge of a low stool behind him, and crashed to the floor.

I reached the door and yanked on the knob.

The door didn't open. I had seen Harold close it, but I hadn't realized he had locked it. I knew now that must have been the double clicking sound I'd heard. He had already engaged the lock before pushing it shut.

I wracked my brain, trying to think what I should do next. But my mind went blank, gripped in panic. I kept pulling at the door, and began shouting for help, even though I knew there was no one to hear.

A scuffling sound from behind caught my attention. I spun back to face Harold.

He was on his feet again, a look of thunderous rage on his face. In his hand was the brick, removed from my purse now, with the plastic baggy still around it. He raised the weapon over his head and charged at me.

What happened next seemed to unfold in slow motion. I saw Harold running at me. Then a movement near the ceiling drew my eye. The large, ornate chandelier hanging in the centre of the room was wreathed in a swirling blur, almost like a white fog. The chandelier began shaking and burst loose from the ceiling at the exact second Harold was about to step beneath it.

He must have heard the creaking noise overhead, because he slowed and looked up. His eyes widened in an expression of horror as the chandelier broke loose from the ceiling. His momentum wouldn't allow him to stop short of being struck by the falling fixture. Instead, he swerved to the side.

The chandelier crashed to the floor very close to Harold.

His face white, Harold stood on the spot, looking from

me to the shattered chandelier and back again, the brick still upraised in his hand. Recovering from his confusion, he made an uncertain move toward me again, walking over the broken glass.

But he'd only come a few steps forward when, suddenly, the foggy blur shot down from the ceiling and across the room at him. Instantly, Harold was flying backwards through the air, his feet off the ground.

I squinted, trying to make sense of what I was seeing.

Harold's body shot backwards toward the large window in the near wall. As he connected with the glass, I saw a flash of ghostly white hands shoving against his shoulders, propelling him backwards. Harold smashed through the glass, creating a booming sound, followed by delicate tinkling noises, as thousands of shards of glass rained onto the hardwood floor.

Harold disappeared out the window, his scream moving away from me until it cut off abruptly with a crash as he must have struck the ground below. The white fog had rushed out the window with him, leaving me alone.

My inertia broke and I ran to look out. Harold lay on the ground below. Even from here, I could see his neck was twisted at an impossible angle. Of the fog, there was no sign. It had seemingly faded away on the evening wind.

"Thank you, Frank," I whispered into the gathering darkness.

There was no response, but I had expected none. Frank had got what he wanted. His work here was done.

I went to my discarded purse and pulled my cell phone out. With shaking hands, I dialled the number for the police station and quickly explained to Tucker what had happened. I was only halfway through the story when

Tucker cut me off, sounding more firm and efficient than he usually did.

"Emma? Are you in any danger?"

"Not anymore," I replied.

"Then sit tight. I'm on my way."

The line went dead in my ear.

17

In the aftermath of the danger, Tucker remained unusually helpful. He arrived on the scene within minutes of my call and listened calmly as I explained what had happened. I barely managed to find the words to explain Harold Abbott's last moments, but Tucker reassured me that it would be fine.

"Look up there," he said. "Seems like our friend Mr. Abbott was a might bit paranoid."

I looked up to where he pointed and saw a tiny dot of red light in the corner of the room. I started, surprised that Tucker had spotted something I had missed. The room had CCTV.

Evidently, Harold's paranoia about visitors stealing from him during the tours had worked out in my favor. His confession was surely caught on camera, although I suspected the ghostly blur that had attacked him would remain invisible in the recording. To anyone else watching the tape, it would just seem as though Harold had suddenly lost his mind and leaped backward out the window for no reason.

The next couple of hours passed quickly, or maybe it only seemed quick because my head was still spinning from all that had occurred.

I accompanied Tucker to the station to give an official statement. Whether he knew he was breaking all kinds of rules and didn't care, or whether he didn't know there were rules, I wasn't sure, but he let me watch the footage with him before I gave my statement.

It caused me a lot of embarrassment when the recording showed me returning the stolen paperweight, but Tucker seemed to understand and believe me when I told him why I had it. He didn't comment on whether or not it had been unwise of me to steal what I had initially mistaken for a murder weapon.

As Harold Abbott's final moments began to play out, I wanted to look away but I couldn't. I had to see, had to know. I watched as the chandelier started to shake and then came loose. Harold moved to the side, more force in the movement that I had originally seen. He stumbled and his arms pin-wheeled as he moved backwards. The momentum caught him and his feet lifted off the ground. He slammed into the window, and then I did look away.

As I had expected, there was no sign of any ghostly hands on the footage. But I knew what I had seen and I knew Frank's ghost had saved me.

I asked Tucker what he thought had caused the chandelier to fall. He shrugged and told me it was probably already loose and pure luck had made it come crashing down in that moment. I wasn't buying it, but I wasn't about to argue with him and make him question things. He would think I was crazy.

I gave my statement then, leaving out the parts that the average person wouldn't believe.

Afterward, Tucker drove me home, where I faced the concern of my grandparents when I confessed I had been investigating a killer. But beneath their worry, I could see they were proud of me for getting justice for Frank Clarkson.

There was no need for me to add that I had been asked to investigate by the ghost of Frank himself. They knew I had ghostly visions, but there was no reason to upset them with details about what those visions wanted from me.

18

I returned to work at the Christmas Garden the next day. Grandma tried to talk me out of it, saying I might be in shock, but I reassured her I was fine and that hanging around the house would only drive me crazy. Eventually, she relented, but she insisted on coming with me.

She spent the afternoon and the early evening telling anyone who would listen, and some who made it clear they didn't want to hear, that her granddaughter had solved a murder and almost been killed. Of course she embellished the story, and before long I was being painted as some sort of action hero.

But I didn't really mind. Everyone knew the story was exaggerated, and if it made Grandma happy, then so be it.

～

IT WAS on my second day back at the park that I saw Betty Blackwell approaching me with a face like thunder.

I groaned inside. What was her problem now?

"You lied to me," she accused me as she stepped up to the raffle table I was manning.

"Excuse me?" I said.

That wasn't what I had been expecting at all. I was waiting for the latest problem, like how I had been five minutes late that day.

"You told me you needed to leave the park early the day before yesterday because your grandma needed something. But you went on the historical tour instead."

"I most certainly did not lie," I replied, trying my best to sound indignant. "I had to pick up Grandma's Christmas blouse from the dry cleaners. It would have been closed if I had stayed here all evening. And then I went on the tour after that, yes, but that's not the reason I left early."

More lies. Betty bought it, though, and her face softened.

"Oh, I'm sorry for being such a grouch. You did a good thing, Emma. And if you fancy cracking another mystery..."

She trailed off and I frowned. I was pretty sure that was an apology and it threw me. I caught myself and nodded.

"Umm, sure. What's up?"

Betty said, "The lights were vandalised again yesterday and we're still no closer to working out who is responsible. The damage has been repaired, but it's costing us a lot of money to keep replacing broken lights. I wondered if you'd maybe patrol the trees and see if you can spot anything untoward."

I was pretty sure it was kids, or even wild racoons or something, wrecking the lights once the park was closed for the day. But if it would put Betty's mind at rest to have someone on watch, then I decided I might as well do it. The snow was coming down again and it was a freezing cold day. Walking through the trees would be a bit warmer than just sitting here.

"I'd be happy to take a look. But what about the raffle?" I asked.

Betty actually smiled. "I can take over that," she said. "I quite enjoyed it the other day."

Was Betty thawing? My question was met with a resounding *no* at her next statement.

"Besides, I'm the only one here who can do it right. You and the others don't pressure people enough to buy tickets, so we never make any money."

I bit back my smile and stood up. With a nod to Betty, I headed for the trees.

I HAD BEEN WALKING AROUND for about half an hour and I felt a whole lot warmer than I had at the table, but my fingers were still cold, even through the woollen gloves Grandma had knitted for me. I decided to head back into the main square and grab a cup of hot chocolate.

As I made my way towards the square, I saw a flicker of green moving through the trees.

I gasped. It was her, the woman in the green coat. I abandoned my plan to go for hot chocolate and followed the woman. I was a good distance behind her, and by the time I caught up to her, she was already pulling strings of lights back out of the trees.

"What do you think you're doing?" I demanded.

She turned to face me, her arms weighed down with strands of lights and her face a mask of guilt. I was surprised to see she was around the same age as me. I was expecting her to be a teenager, judging by her actions. But her eyes looked older, like they had seen too much. They were underlined with black shadows that she'd clumsily tried to hide with concealer.

"I found the lights on the ground. I was trying to help," she said, tossing shoulder-length dark hair out of her eyes.

"No, you weren't," I disagreed. "You were pulling them down. And this isn't the first time, is it? I also saw you destroy part of the mural a few days ago. Give me one good reason why I shouldn't march you over to the deputy on duty and have you arrested."

The woman's pale face crumpled and tears began to pour down her cheeks.

"Please don't do that. I'm sorry. I just ... I just couldn't bear it. I had to do something to get the event shut down. I just had to."

I frowned. There was more to this than someone intent on ruining a community event. I decided I wanted to know more before I turned the woman in.

"Let's go," I said. "It's cold here. We'll get some hot chocolate and you can explain."

She looked up in surprise. "You mean you're not going to call security?"

I shrugged. "That depends on whether or not you tell me the truth," I replied.

She glanced down at the lights still clutched in her hands. "What about these?"

"I suggest you put them back where you found them."

She nodded and began to restring the lights. I watched her as she worked. She was methodical and she got the lights back up pretty quickly. It was hard to watch her and not help, but I reminded myself the strands were only down because she had pulled them down. She wore a strange expression as she worked. Sombre, but with flashes of a sad smile, as she rubbed the odd bulb here and there between her fingers.

She finished and we walked back into the square where I ordered two cups of hot chocolate and escorted the woman in the green coat to a quiet area where we sat down side by side.

"Why don't you start by telling me your name," I said.

"Beth," she replied.

"Okay, Beth. Why did you try to ruin the Christmas Garden?"

Her eyes filled with tears again, but this time, she managed to blink them back before they could spill over.

"It's about my son, Harley. Christmas was always his favorite holiday. He would spend weeks looking forward to the Christmas Garden. As soon as the dark nights started creeping in, it was all he would talk about. Last year, we came every day. You should have seen how happy he was. His eyes would light up with joy at the lights and the decorations, no matter how many times he had seen them before."

She stopped and I was ready to ask her what that had to do with anything when she looked down into her cup and started talking again.

"He became very sick over the summer. I was told there was nothing the doctors could do, other than trying to keep him out of pain. He had a couple of months, they said. I prayed he'd somehow live to see another Christmas, but sadly, he didn't. He was taken from me only a few months ago."

"That's terrible. I'm so sorry," I said, feeling my expression soften.

She nodded her thanks and continued. "The day the Christmas Garden opened, I walked by the park. I heard children's laughter and shrieks of delight. It sickened me to know that my Harley would never laugh again, never enjoy the magic of another Christmas. I know it sounds stupid, but it was our thing, mine and Harley's. If he couldn't enjoy it, then why should anyone else? I knew I had to do something, and I planned to get the Garden shut down."

"So you turned to vandalism to make that happen?" I prompted.

She bit her lip. "When the old man who took care of the reindeer was killed, I figured that would be the end of the Christmas Garden this year. But it wasn't, so I felt I had to keep coming back until it was all stopped."

She fell silent a moment and then turned to me with a sad smile. "So, yeah. I'm just a bitter woman who wanted to spoil Christmas for everyone. If you want to have me arrested, do it. It's not like you could make me feel any worse."

I shook my head. "Beth, I can't imagine what all that must have been like for you. I'm not going to turn you in. I think you've suffered enough."

"Thank you," she said. "And for what it's worth, I won't do it again. I'll keep away. Saying it out loud like that, it made me realize how stupid I've been. Ruining Christmas for other families isn't going to bring Harley back, and it's the last thing he would have wanted me to do. He loved the Christmas Garden so much."

An idea came to me and I studied Beth's face for a moment. "I have a thought. Will you hear me out?"

"Sure." Beth nodded.

"Instead of avoiding the park, why don't you help out? We're always looking for volunteers, and it would be a way for you to feel close to Harley again. It would give you the chance to do something positive in his memory and help other children feel the same magic he did when he was here."

"I ... I don't know," she said hesitantly.

I waved my hand in front of us, gesturing toward the main square of the park.

"Look around you, Beth. These kids love Christmas like Harley did. It would be a lovely tribute to his life to volunteer in the place that brought him so much pleasure."

A slow smile crossed Beth's face and she nodded.

"You know something? I think you're right. I can see Harley in these kids, and instead of making me sad, it makes me happy to think that something he loved so much will continue to go on and make other kids as happy as he was."

"Come on then, let's go get you signed up," I said. "Oh, best not to mention to Betty Blackwell, the event's coordinator this year, that you're the one responsible for the vandalism. She's not a very forgiving lady."

Beth nodded and we walked across the square towards the marquee.

"I'm Emma, by the way," I told her, suddenly realizing I hadn't introduced myself.

We entered the marquee then and found Betty Blackwell back in the warmth with her clipboard.

"This is Beth. She'd like to volunteer to help out," I said.

Betty's eyes narrowed as she took in our new volunteer. "I've seen you around. Beth Wilkins, isn't it?" she asked.

"That's right." Beth nodded uncertainly.

"About time you caught her," Betty told me.

My mouth dropped open. "I ... what do you mean?" I asked.

"She's been vandalizing the lights and decorations since day one," Betty said. "And it took you this long to figure it out."

Beth and I exchanged a glance. Beth looked like she wanted the ground to open up and swallow her.

But Betty only tut-tutted in her direction.

"Now, we'll have none of that. The children here expect us to be happy and cheery, my dear."

We both look at her, locked in shocked silence.

Betty tutted again and explained to Beth, "Isn't it obvious? I knew it was you from the beginning. And I had heard about what happened with your little boy, so I had a feeling I knew why you were trying to shut down the Christmas Garden. I wanted to reach out to you, but I suspected you wouldn't listen to a cranky old woman like me. I figured Emma here might just get through to you."

"But if you knew who it was, why did you tell Sheriff Tucker to look into it?" I asked.

"Because I knew he would never work it out, but I had to look like I was doing something to find the culprit."

She turned her attention back to Beth. "I understand what it's like to lose a child and I realize that feeling can make otherwise good people do things that are out of character."

A shadow of grief passed over Betty's face. She cleared her throat. "Now, enough chitchat. Let's get on, shall we? Beth dear, why don't you shadow Emma for today and learn the ropes?"

I did exactly what she suggested, and spent the rest of the day showing our newest volunteer her responsibilities.

19

"I don't think I'll ever be able to move again," Grandpa said, rubbing his stomach and sighing dramatically.

"That'll teach you about wanting extra helpings." Grandma grinned, clearly pleased that her Christmas dinner had once more proved too delicious to leave any behind. She winked at me, then turned back to Grandpa. "If you're that full, you won't be wanting any Christmas pudding then?"

"Are you insane, woman? Of course I want Christmas pudding. Lots of it," he replied.

We all laughed. It had been a lovely morning. We had shared our well wishes and exchanged gifts, and then Grandma had insisted on making the dinner alone. I offered to help, but she shooed me away, telling me Christmas dinner was her thing and it always would be. I gave up in the end, because it was clear I was just getting in her way.

Grandpa and I had gone to the living room and sat chatting. Even Grandpa had Christmas day off. Of course, he'd been out to feed the animals and check things were all good, but that was it.

We'd shared laughter and happiness, and Grandma's Christmas pudding with brandy sauce was the final piece to make the day absolutely perfect. Even Snowball had enjoyed scraps from the table. I could swear she looked fatter already as she lay in the corner of the kitchen and bleated softly until she fell asleep.

"You'll be leaving soon, huh?" Grandpa asked me.

I looked at my new watch, a gift from Grandma and Grandpa, and nodded.

"Yes. I'll have time to help with the dishes and then Billy will be picking me up. I told Suzy we'd be at her and Brian's place around four."

"It's Christmas, Emma. You won't be doing any dishes," Grandma said.

"But you cooked," I insisted.

She smiled. "Yes. And I'll clean too. Now go and have a nap or something. Sleep all of that turkey off."

I did as I was told. I was so stuffed and so tired I didn't have the energy to argue with her. Anyway, I would be awful company for my friends tonight if I didn't have a nap.

I woke up in time to fix my hair and mascara and reapply my lip gloss, and then Billy was outside, honking his horn. I called out my goodbyes and picked up my bag of gifts for Suzy, Billy, and Brian.

I walked out to the car, feeling like a bag of nerves. I hadn't seen Billy since the night I ran out on him, although we'd had a long phone call where I finally explained to him that I'd been investigating the death of Frank Clarkson. The ghost of Frank I kept to myself, of course. No sense complicating the story, especially since the ghost had been satisfied and faded away for good once the truth of the murder was out.

Billy hadn't been thrilled with my putting myself in danger, or with the fact that I hadn't been open with him about why I'd needed that "bloody" paperweight examined. I had worried he was angry with me.

But now, he smiled warmly when he saw me heading his way and that made me think maybe it would all be okay after all.

20

T*ink. Tink. Tink.*

Brian clinked his spoon against his cider mug, signalling for silence. Immediately, Billy and I smothered our laughter at Suzy's latest joke and quieted down. The four of us had been enjoying Christmas desserts in front of the warm fireplace, when Brian had broken up the conversation.

"If you two hyenas will stop cackling for a minute," Brian said, with a mock stern look at Billy and me, "my lovely wife has an announcement to make."

"Thank you, my always thoughtful husband." Suzy's eyes sparkled with mischief as she found herself the centre of attention.

"What is it? What's the announcement?" Billy asked.

"Yeah, c'mon already. Spill it, Suzy," I added.

"Well, if y'all are gonna be that impatient, I might just keep the news to myself," she teased.

Billy and I groaned.

But as much as Suzy was enjoying torturing us with her secret, it was obvious she also couldn't hold it in any longer.

"I'm pregnant," she burst out with a grin. "Not quite three months on and we haven't told anybody yet, but you two are our best friends, so we wanted you to be the first to know."

"Pregnant?" I gave a happy shriek and Suzy shrieked with me, and then we were all laughing and talking at once.

"When's this baby arriving?" Billy asked.

"The due date is early May," Brian answered proudly.

"And you'll be the godparents, of course," Suzy said.

"Of course," I agreed. "We'd be insulted if we weren't."

We all laughed and pulled our chairs closer around the fire, while Brian prepared us more celebratory toasts of apple cider.

"Wow, I didn't see that one coming, did you?" Billy asked as he put the car into drive and headed away from Suzy's place.

I swivelled in my seat and waved to Suzy and Brian, who waved back from their doorstep.

"What do you mean?" I asked as we rounded the bend, leaving the happy couple behind, and I turned back to the front. I was kidding. Of course I knew exactly what he meant.

"Suzy being pregnant," he said.

I laughed and shook my head.

"What?" he smiled.

"I admit I didn't have a clue until they announced it, although I should have guessed, what with how Suzy's eating habits have changed and the way she's been avoiding heavy work. But how did you not see it? You're the doctor around here."

He looked sheepish. "Well, maybe it was dense of me

not to notice the signs. But to tell the truth, it isn't exactly Suzy I've had my eye on these days."

I blushed and looked out the window at the blanket of snow, not displeased at the comment.

Maybe it was time we finally stopped skating around the subject. I had fought being romantically linked with Billy ever since coming back to Hillbilly Hollow. And yet, when I had faced my death in Harold Abbott's house so recently, suddenly I had known. I had realized the greatest tragedy in losing my life so suddenly would be losing what might have been—the chance to explore a possible future with the man I cared for above all others.

We drove the rest of the way to the farm in comfortable silence, until Billy pulled into the driveway in front of the darkened farmhouse. From the looks of it, my grandparents had already gone off to bed.

I made to open the door and Billy put his hand on my wrist, stopping me.

"Emma, I've wanted to say this for a long time, but I've kept putting it off, telling myself I'm happy just to have you back in my life. But the truth is, it's not enough for me. I don't want us to just be friends anymore. I want us to be more than that."

"What are you saying?" I asked quietly, although I knew the answer full well.

"I'm saying it's time we stop pretending and move this thing we both know is between us forward. It's time we make it official. Beginning this Friday with an actual, not-just-friends-now date. And yes, I know I sound like we're back in junior high, but...I want you to be my girlfriend. Will you?"

I couldn't stop a grin from creeping across my face, and I

could see my own nervous excitement mirrored in his expression.

"Yes. I'd love to," I said.

He breathed an audible sigh of relief and then he laughed and I found myself joining in. This had been a long time coming.

I started to lean toward him then.

Suddenly, a bright light switched on above the driveway, flooding the hood of the car with a golden glare.

"Emma? Is that you out there?" my grandma's voice called from the doorway.

It seemed everybody wasn't quite down for the night after all. I could see Grandma's pale form dressed in a night-gown, hovering like a ghost just inside the front door.

I cracked my door and shouted, "Coming, Grandma. You go on up to bed."

She must have heard me, because the light over the driveway switched off and she disappeared from the doorway.

"I'd better go," I told Billy. "Good night."

"I'll call you," he said as I got out of the car.

I stood and watched as he drove away. But I didn't make a move to go inside. Not just yet. Instead, I stood in place and looked up at the sky. It was a clear night and I smiled as I watched the stars twinkling above me, spreading their magic.

It was all happening now. Things were coming together for me. I was glad I had finally plucked up the courage to take a chance and say yes to Billy. It might mean the end of our friendship as it stood, but it wasn't just an end. It was the start of a new chapter. Here. Together. And that was as magical as Christmas, the snow, and the stars all put together.

A nudging against my leg pulled my attention away from the stars and I crouched down and scratched Snowball's head behind her ears. She must have crept out from her favourite hiding spot under the front porch. She bleated in pleasure, craning her neck forward to get closer to me.

"We're all moving forward, Snowball," I whispered to her. "And I have a feeling next year will be the best one yet."

It was true. Suzy and Brian were going to have a baby, and if that wasn't a major step forward, then I didn't know what was. It would be a learning curve for sure, but I knew Suzy would nail it. She could do anything she put her mind to, and I knew she would throw herself into motherhood whole heartedly. It didn't mean she wouldn't make mistakes along the way. She wouldn't be Suzy if she didn't get into a few hilarious mishaps, but I knew she would be a great mom, and Brian would make a great dad too.

And then there was Billy and I, taking a big step forward, moving toward a future that I couldn't quite picture. But that didn't matter. Not knowing exactly where we were headed was all part of the fun.

I realized in that moment that I had a lot to pause and be thankful for. I had solved the mystery of the woman in the green coat, and Beth and I had become friends. I had also solved Frank's murder and gotten justice for another ghost.

I was happy with the conclusion the two mysteries had arrived at, but I also knew I wasn't really standing at an end point. I was at a beginning.

Continue following the ghostly mysteries and eccentric characters of Hillbilly Hollow in "Terrible Tidings in Hillbilly Hollow."

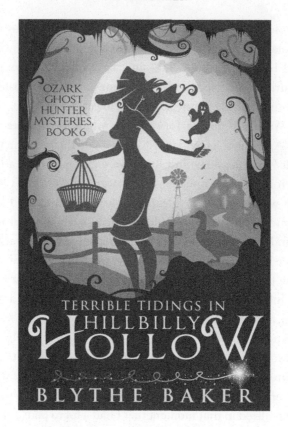

ABOUT THE AUTHOR

Blythe Baker is a thirty-something bottle redhead from the South Central part of the country. When she's not slinging words and creating new worlds and characters, she's acting as chauffeur to her children and head groomer to her household of beloved pets.

Blythe enjoys long walks with her dog on sweaty days, grubbing in her flower garden, cooking, and ruthlessly de-cluttering her overcrowded home. She also likes binge-watching mystery shows on TV and burying herself in books about murder.

To learn more about Blythe, visit her website and sign up for her newsletter at www.blythebaker.com

Made in the USA
Las Vegas, NV
11 February 2023

67349880R00094